BRANDED

ALSO BY LARAMIE BRISCOE

The Haldonia Monarchy

Royal Rebel

Royal Chaos

Royal Love

USA TODAY AND *WSJ* BESTSELLING AUTHOR

LARAMIE BRISCOE

Branded
Paperback Edition

Love N. Books Press
An Imprint of Wolfpack Publishing
1707 E. Diana Street
Tampa, FL 33610

www.lovenbookspress.com

Edited by My Brother's Editor
Cover Design by Pilcrow Design

Paperback ISBN 979-8-89567-723-0
Ebook ISBN 979-8-89567-722-3

BRANDED

ONE
ATLEE

I DON'T RECOGNIZE the face staring back at me. There's no way it can be mine. A purple bruise covers a good portion of the right side, and my lip is split. My hair hurts where the robber must have grabbed himself a handful. I don't remember it, but that's the only thing I can think of.

Shame flutters in my stomach. This isn't my fault, and it's not as if I asked to be hit, but the shame is still there.

"Are you going to work today?" The deep voice belongs to Devlin Nelson. It sends goose bumps along my arms and up my neck. It isn't like it's the first time I've heard him speak, or even the first time he's spoken close to my ear. It is, however, the first time he's sounded irritated and angry on my behalf.

"No," I whisper, shaking my head. "I don't want anyone to see me like this."

He grunts as his gaze travels my face. "People should see you, see what that motherfucker did to you, but that's your decision."

I swallow roughly. "I especially don't want my sister to see me. Thank you for bringing me here."

"Wasn't like I was about to let you go anywhere else last night."

Glancing around, I realize we're in a small house. I always assumed Devlin lived with the rest of his brothers in the big house on the property. It's at the forefront of my mind, and I have to ask the question. "Do you live by yourself?"

He was speaking, and I interrupted him. With a shake of his head and a grin, he inhales deeply. "Yeah. I'm the oldest, and there's no way I'm living with my little brothers as an adult. Already did that. Built this place on my own. It's not much, but it's mine."

"Is it still on the Nelson land?"

"Yeah, we're about half a mile from the main house. Not too far, but far enough that we aren't up each other's asses."

He's never spoken to me at length like this, and I'm learning more about him in this conversation than I've ever known. "Is that important to you? To have privacy?" I raise my eyebrows at him. "For all your women?" My heart pounds against my ribs as I wait for him to answer.

"All my women?" He runs a hand through his hair. "You think I'm bringing a bunch of women out here?"

I shrug, pulling my zip-up jacket tighter around me. "I don't know. There isn't a lot I know about you, but I do wonder if I'm fucking up whatever it might be that you have going."

"If there was a chance of you fucking something up, do you think I would've brought you out here?"

I don't know. "Maybe you feel sorry for me?"

Reaching forward, his thumb and forefinger grip my chin

lightly. He pulls it down so that our eyes meet one another. He licks his lips and clicks his tongue. "There are a lot of things I feel for you, Atlee. Sorry isn't one of 'em."

I fucking melt into the floor. No man my age is out here saying these things to me. I'm lucky if they even remember my name after the first swipe and text message. I never thought I'd have a crush on an older man, but here we are. "Oh, yeah?" I tilt my head to the side. "What's one of those things you feel for me?" Call me a glutton for punishment, but my body hurts, and my face is bruised. I need a win, and if I've gotta ask for it, then I will.

He clears his throat, grunting a little. Pulling his bottom lip between his teeth, his white teeth chomp down, and he groans. "Fuck, Atlee. You don't wanna know."

"I do," I plead. "Look, what happened last night really shook me. I need a win. I need to know that I'm gonna come out on the other side of this, because right now? I'm not sure I'm going to."

"You are." He moves his hand from my chin, cupping my cheek with his palm. "I'm going to make sure you do." He swallows hard, his Adam's apple moving up and down with it. "And if I have to tell you the shit I've been thinkin' about you in order to make sure you know, then that's what I'll do."

My cheeks heat as I realize what he's saying. He has been thinking about me, and he's about to give me the win I've asked for. "Don't lay it on too thick, Devlin. Then I won't believe you."

He grins, the sides of his lips curving up. "Since the night you and I rode together when Truett was injured, I've done nothing but think about you. In a friendly way, in a not-so-friendly way. In any of the ways I can think about you, I've thought about you. Whether I should or not, whether it keeps me up at night or not." He shoves his free hand through his hair. "More nights than I care to admit, I'm lying in there." He tilts his head toward what I've learned is his bedroom. "Thinking about you."

My heart is thudding, and I'm breathless as I lean in closer, wanting to know what else he's going to say. "What are you thinking?" I whisper, hanging on to his every word.

"Shit..." He reaches forward with his free hand and tugs me to him, holding me close. "Every single thing I shouldn't be thinking about you. You're too young, but it doesn't stop me from wondering what you look like without your clothes on. What you would sound like if my lips tugged on what I imagine are cherry red nipples. If you get a hitch in your breath when you come."

I close my eyes and inhale sharply. Men—boys, really—my age don't talk like this. At least not to me. I've wanted them to, but never knew how to ask for it, and hoped I wouldn't have to. If anyone were to ever talk about me, they wouldn't say that I'm confident.

I'm not.

But I do know what I want, and Devlin Nelson ticks every single one of my boxes. Before last night, I would never have done what I'm about to do. Now though? Now I know what it's like to worry that you won't make it through a shift, what it's like to wonder if someone will come find you in time. So I'm not willing to push my luck anymore. I'm not willing to settle back and wait for the person who's supposed to make my blood rush through my veins.

The Atlee who woke up today is more than willing to do whatever it takes to make this shit happen.

Which is why I step forward so that our bodies touch. His strong, big one pressed up against mine. Looking forward, the only thing I can see is his chest. The one he held me against when he came to save me. Rolling my lips together, I lift my head, my eyes meeting his. What I see there is enough to make my heart pound. It's full of interest, desire, and something darker. Something I'm not willing to think about too much, because I've heard things about the Nelson brothers.

Reaching up, I wrap my arms around his neck, digging my fingers into his hair. I hold him to me as I stand on my tiptoes and press my lips to his.

He groans in the back of his throat, standing there like a statue, and I'm about to lose my nerve when he inhales deeply and slips his arms around my waist. Pulling back, he leans down, dropping his forehead to mine. "Do you know what you're doing here, Atlee?"

Closing my eyes, I nod before using my tongue to collect his taste off my lips. "Yeah."

"You've had a rough twenty-four hours. You think this is a good idea?" His deep voice causes goose bumps to pop up over my arms.

"Might not be a good idea, Devlin, but it's what I need." I open my eyes and look into his.

The dark depths flare with passion and intensity. His hand leaves my waist, moving down to cup the curve of my ass. "I'll always give you what you need, Atlee. All you have to do is ask. But I'm definitely gonna need you to ask, especially after what happened last night."

Asking has been hard for me, but if there's one thing I know, it's that I want this. I want this more than I've ever wanted anything in my life. "Devlin?" I start. "Make me forget what happened. Make me feel safe again. Please?"

Just like that, he palms my ass, lifting me up, and walks me over to his bed. When he tosses me down, I know he's about to wreck me for any other man that might come after him.

TWO
DEVLIN

ATLEE WALSH IS the hottest piece of ass I've seen in a long time. Since the moment I met her, she's had me intrigued. Little did I think anything like this would be happening right now, though. My conscience is screaming at me that I shouldn't be taking advantage of the situation, but my body is saying I should give her exactly what she's asking for.

Once I get us over to the bed, I toss her down and cover her body with mine. She's smaller than other women I've previously been with. It doesn't mean I wanted them more than I wanted her, but I'm slightly terrified I might crush her with the weight of my body.

"Don't take it easy on me," she says, her light eyes looking into mine.

There's a part of me that wants to listen to her. There's another part that wants to take and own. It wants to give her every single thing I've needed for myself. "I'll take you however I can get you, Atlee. I've been obsessed with you since the first time we met."

"Have you?" she questions, her legs coming up to my hips.

I grunt in the back of my throat. "How in the hell have you not been able to tell?"

She shoves her hand through my hair, tugging so that our faces are millimeters apart. I feel all of it in my cock. It jumps against the zipper on my jeans, crowding into the space between my body and the clothing.

"No one's ever been obsessed with me before." She shrugs. "I thought you were just trying to be nice."

A chuckle works its way out of my throat. "Trust me, I'm not nice to anyone, but…" I trail my finger along her jawline and down her throat, hooking my finger in her T-shirt, yanking it to expose her chest. "I might be nice to you." Dipping my head down, I take her lips with mine, tangling our tongues together.

Our hands travel each other's bodies, mapping the terrain over our clothing. My fingers are punishing against the globes of her ass as I cup the material of her jeans and pull her closer to me. Ripping my lips from hers, I suck in a breath. "Atlee, you're sure about this, right?"

"Don't fuckin' ask me again," she says, reaching down to take the hem of her shirt and pulling it over her head.

I move back to give her enough room to throw the shirt to the side. My gaze takes in her flat stomach and stacked tits held up by the lace of her bra. My hands bracket her waist before meeting in the middle and unbuttoning the clasp of her jeans. Pulling down the material, I take it off the end of her feet and toss it to the side, leaving her in nothing but her bra and panties.

"You're fucking gorgeous, Atlee. This smooth skin, tight tits, and stomach that flares into these hips? Why do you hide this?"

She runs her gaze down my body. "Same reason you hide what I imagine is a very fit body behind your clothes too. Because you don't want people to look at you like you're a piece of meat."

"If it were you..." I reach up to yank my T-shirt over the back of my head and throw it on top of hers. "I'd let you look at me like a piece of meat any day of the week."

Her nostrils flare as her gaze travels down my chest and ab muscles, taking in the ink that I started getting the night before I joined the military. I've added to it over the years, sometimes things that mean something to me, others that don't. She licks her lips. "Are you going to take those jeans off?"

The tension between us is thick, and my heart is pounding a rhythm against my chest, my cock pulsing as I think about what's going to happen once I get these jeans off and there's very little between us. "Once these come off, I'm not going to be able to stop myself when it comes to you."

"Good. I'm waiting on you, Devlin."

That's all I need to push them down, and then cover her body with mine again. Wrapping my hand in her hair, I tug it back, exposing her throat to my mouth. Attacking it, I kiss, lick, suck, and nip at her pulse. Her fingers tangle in my hair, holding me to the base of her throat, encouraging me to take the flesh between my teeth.

"Devlin, that feels so fucking good."

Her thighs spread wide, bracketing my hips, and she presses her pussy up into my cock. It's hot and hard, trying to escape the confines of my boxer briefs.

"I'm ready to make you feel even better," I whisper as I pull back from her neck and move down her chest, pulling the straps of her bra along her arms, releasing the round globes from the material and exposing the skin to my gaze. "Look at those nipples, Atlee. Peaked and ready for my mouth. Is that okay with you?"

She scissors her legs against me. "Yes, I'm dying for you to touch me."

I'm dying to touch her in the way I want to too. Leaning forward, I take a nipple between my teeth, tugging, before I soothe the ache with my tongue. She moans in the back of her throat, sending a shot of arousal through the middle of my body. My cock jumps, pre-cum leaking against the fabric of my boxer briefs.

Her hand snakes down between us, slipping beneath the waistband and wrapping her fingers around my length. Her palm circles the head before sliding down to the root, starting to jack me off. I let her play for as long as I dare before grabbing her wrist and pressing her arm up over her head. Pulling my mouth from her nipple, I move down her body, trailing my tongue over her flesh, letting it dip into her belly button before I kneel at the edge of the bed. My fingertips grasp hold of her panties and yank them down her legs.

"Devlin, what are you doing?"

Hooking her legs over my shoulders, I give her a grin. "If you don't know what I'm doing, then the boys you've been dating are even worse than I thought."

Her hand moves to the concave of her stomach, and she presses her fingernails into her flesh. "Guys my age aren't really down for doing anything that doesn't benefit them."

"They don't know that this would benefit them?" I raise an eyebrow, leaning forward and blowing on her pussy.

She shivers, and that reaction is everything I've been waiting for. "They only want one thing, and that's for themselves to feel good. Hardly any of them think about the other person in the situation."

"Then you're in luck, because I'd cut off my left nut before I let a woman not be satisfied after I fuck her." She squeals when I press my mouth to her pussy, using my tongue to go after her clit, and then press two fingers into her. She's wet, wetter than I imagined she would be, and so fucking tight, I'm not sure if I'll be able to get my dick wet the first time or not. Her legs tighten around my ears, and she thrusts up into me, obviously wanting more.

Closing my eyes, I let myself go in nose first, licking and sucking, fingers pushing in and pulling out. She's riding my tongue, her body tight as a string. My cock sticks out in front of me, and I reach down with my free hand to give it a few tugs. I can't wait to get inside her, but I want her tight and slightly satisfied first.

Her hands reach out beside her and grip the cover in her fingers, pulling on it tightly as she screams her pleasure. Not for the first time, it makes me glad I live here by myself and not at the big house with my brothers. "There ya go," I encourage her. "Ride it out, Atlee."

Her body shakes as she does what I've told her to, her chest rising and falling, and her eyes looking down at me. They're glazed over with satisfaction, which is exactly what I wanted. Reaching up, I hook my hand behind her neck and bring her gaze to mine. "Condom or not, Atlee. Your decision. I'm clean, and it's been a while for me."

"No condom, Devlin. I wanna feel you. Wanna feel alive and forget everything that happened last night."

And I want to give her all of that. Pushing off my knees, I cover her body with mine before reaching down and spreading her thighs to make room. Using two fingers, I press her open, making sure she's completely ready for me. Her hand comes down, wrapping around my wrist. Our eyes meet.

"I'm ready, Devlin. Fuck me already."

With a groan, I press into her. "You're so fucking tight, goddamn."

"You're so fucking big."

Looking up, she's got a dreamy smile on her face. I put that smile there and gave her that blissed out expression. I'll remember this until the day I die. I've never thought that about any other woman before. Words aren't needed between the two of us as we push and pull, me fucking her swiftly as she shoves her head back against the covers. My hands find hers, our palms connecting before our fingers entwine together. I'm holding on tight as I use the leverage to swing my hips and allow me to get deeper. "Touch yourself," I instruct her between gritted teeth as the tingling starts at the base of my spine.

Her body tightens as she rubs her clit, and I let go of the grip I've had on my pleasure. Reaching down, I take her mouth, and the two of us groan as we crash through our orgasms together. Both of us breathing wildly, I hook my arm around her neck and pull her into me.

"Thank you," she whispers. "Thank you for taking away those bad memories and making me feel safe again."

"You're welcome," I answer.

But in the back of my mind, I'm thinking something else entirely. I'll find the fucker who did this, and I'll make him pay in ways he never thought possible.

THREE
ATLEE

THE NEXT MORNING, I wake up with soreness between my thighs. Devlin ended up taking me twice more before the night was over, and I ended up falling asleep in his bed, right next to him. He's not next to me, but there's a piece of paper on his pillow.

Had to go out and work at Grizzly River. I'll be back tonight. Feel free to make yourself at home.

Reaching over, I grab my phone off the nightstand. I ignored it yesterday and last night while I was with Devlin. When he'd come and gotten me at the pharmacy, I hadn't expected him to bring me to his house. It hadn't even been a thought on my mind. I assumed he would take me home to my apartment. I hadn't imagined he'd bring me here, not when the Nelson brothers are so private about what their home and business look like. There aren't a lot of people here that actually know what the hell is going on out on the Nelson ranch. Opening my phone, I see a few texts from my sister.

Lennon
Atlee, I heard about what happened last night, are you okay? People said they saw you leave with Devlin. Get back to me as soon as possible.

God, I hadn't even thought about texting her to let her know I'm okay. Not that our parents would care. She and I have always been the keepers of each other.

Me
I'm so sorry I didn't text you after everything went down. I was slightly in shock. Even more in shock that Devlin brought me to his house.

Lennon
You're on the Nelson ranch?

She's gonna flip her shit when I tell her this.

Me
I'm not only on the Nelson ranch, but I'm in Devlin's house. He lives separately from the rest of his brothers.

I wait for her to get back to me, but three little dots keep appearing and then disappearing. I know her better than anyone else, so I know she's trying to get her thoughts together. But I'm not surprised when the text comes through.

Lennon
SHUT THE FUCK UP! Atlee, what the hell is happening?!?!?!

Me
I don't know. I was at work, and then someone came in and threatened to rob me. I called Devlin because he told me to call my boss. He came storming in like he was about to save the damn day. Fuck it all if he didn't. He was the hottest thing I've ever seen running in there.

Lennon
I'm sure he did, and I would have loved to have seen him running to save the day. Do you know how hot that is, Atlee? You're living a real-life romance novel right now. You realize that, right?

I inhale deeply, hoping that it'll settle the nervousness in my stomach. While I may be living a real-life romance novel, what got me here is bound to give me nightmares for a while.

Me
Yeah, I just wish I didn't have to look at my face and see what happened to me.

Lennon
What do you mean?

Shit. I didn't realize that she hadn't been told about the violence of the robbery.

Me
What do you know about what happened?

My stomach is full of nerves as I wait for her to answer. I've never been the type of person who liked to call attention to myself, even if I'm not the one doing it. I've always been the one to make myself smaller. It was the easiest way to live in the household where we grew up. We were encouraged to never tell the truth, to always make people feel sorry for us, and to gather sympathy. If we didn't, there were consequences. Now? I find it difficult to be honest without feeling guilty.

Lennon
Just that someone broke in and then Devlin came charging in to save the day. Is that not what happened? I saw Noah at the gas station this morning. He said you were lucky, but didn't mention that anything worse than what I thought went down. Am I wrong?

My hand shakes as I lift my phone up and turn the screen so that I can take a selfie. It takes everything I have to firm my bottom lip up and clear the tears from my eyes, but I don't want her to see me as her small, little sister who she's had to protect her entire life. Quickly, I snap the picture and attach it to the message I'm sending.

Me
I let Payton go home early because there was only about an hour left, and it'd been so slow. A man came in wearing a mask and with a gun. I told him I didn't have the combination to the safe to get the drugs he wanted, and he instructed me to call my boss. I knew Joseph would do nothing except think I was playing a prank on him. Instead of calling him, I called Devlin, who showed up. But not before the guy backhanded me and pulled my hair.

I hit send along with the picture and wait for her. She won't call me. I know she won't. She and I are fully texters. I'll sit here with my phone in my hand, watching the call come through and letting it go straight to voicemail. It takes longer than I expect for the follow-up text.

Lennon
OMG Atlee. Noah didn't say a word about any of this. I'm so sorry this happened to you, and I'm thankful that Devlin was there. Is there anything I can do for you?

Tears pool in my eyes. This is my protector when I didn't have any others. She's always been one of the most important people in my world.

Me
No, I'm safe here. I can lick my wounds, and no one has to see this other than me and Devlin. I have a feeling everyone else was told to stay away.

Lennon
How long do you think you're going to be out there?

Me
Until the bruises fade. Until the questions about what might have happened at the pharmacy die down a little. Probably around a week. Can you do me a favor? Devlin said he's going into town this afternoon, can you give him a bag of my clothes and some toiletries? I don't want to be stuck wearing the same clothes for the week.

Lennon
Will do, but what are you wearing now?

Looking down, I realize I don't want to tell her I'm naked in Devlin's bed. That'll lead to questions I don't want to answer just yet.

Me
One of Devlin's shirts and a pair of his sweatpants. Not entirely the most comfortable thing. I'll appreciate whatever it is you bring me.

Lennon
All right. I'm trusting you because you're an adult, and although I've taken care of you for most of our lives, I have to realize that you're an adult. It's hard for me because you're my favorite person, and I've taken responsibility for you for so long. It kills me that something happened to you and I wasn't around.

Me
As you said, I'm an adult, and you can't be around all the time. I love you, and I'll see you soon.

Lennon
Love you, and send Devlin over here. I'll make sure he gets your stuff. Please be careful and safe.

There's nothing else to say. I'm in the safest place I can be, and for once I'm not scared. For the first time in my life, I can take a full breath and relax.

FOUR
DEVLIN

PULLING up to a stop in front of the Law Offices of Shawn Cooper, I look around as I get out, checking the surroundings. Some things are holdovers from being in the military for as long as I was. Special ops wasn't what I set out for, but it's what found me when I was looking for something to save me after our parents died. Jesse stayed, taking care of everyone, while I left.

I've been trying to make up for it since I came home, but it's not been easy for Jesse to give up some of his control. At the same time, I've been trying to find my place, which is why I didn't think twice about helping Atlee when she called.

Walking up the sidewalk, my stomach clenches. I've never been the type of man who wants to be on the radar of anyone in the legal field, which is crazy considering what we and Truett have been doing, but here I am. I guess I'm proving I'll do anything for Atlee.

That woman has gotten under my skin.

It happened fast.

From the first moment I saw her to the minute she called me to let me know she was in trouble, she intrigued me. No woman has ever intrigued me like that. Not the ones I had one-night stands with in the military, not my high school girlfriend who thought I'd come back to Grizzly River for her. None of them. There's something about those light-blue eyes of hers against the long black hair on her head.

Before I can get to the door, it swings open, and I'm greeted by Lennon. Two sisters never looked so different. Where Atlee has light eyes, dark hair, and curves for days, Lennon has light hair, dark eyes, and is small with not much shape. But those eyes of hers? They're worried.

"Is she okay?" she blurts out immediately.

I nod and push her back toward the entrance so we can take this inside. I'm sure neither one of them really wants their personal business out here in public if they can help it. The Walsh family has a reputation, and these two have done their best to get out from under the cover of that. "She's okay," I assure her as I shut the door. "Is there somewhere we can go to talk privately?"

She nods, turning to walk down a hallway, then peels off into what appears to be a conference room. "Atlee sent me a picture." She wrings her hands in front of her. "Her face looks bad."

"Yeah," I agree. "He did a number on her, but her spirit is there. It's still kicking. He didn't break it."

Her laugh is hollow. "It would take more than a man like that to break either one of our spirits, considering how we grew up. I'm worried about her, though. There were things that happened in her childhood—she may not remember them, but this might bring them up. Please be on the lookout for that. Did the guy who hurt her get out of jail?"

I'm not supposed to know anything about the guy, but I have my sources, and I've put them to good use. "He's held on bond. I don't think he, or anyone he knows, will be able to get him out. Nobody's touching her while she's under my care either, so you don't have anything to worry about."

Her body deflates as she lets out a breath. Going over to a corner, she grabs two bags and brings them over to me. "She asked for some things to wear and toiletries. I think I got everything she may need, including her laptop." Lennon pushes a piece of hair back from her face, and her eyes pin mine. "I know she's staying with you, and I don't want her to get bored."

Memories of last night flow through my mind. "She is, and as soon as she's ready, I'll bring her home. I just don't think it's a good idea for her to stay by herself."

There's tension between her sister and me as Lennon tilts her head to the side. "How do you know she lives by herself?"

Fuck. "I make it my business to know most of what goes on in this town. It's good to be prepared." There's no reason to tell her that Atlee and I have been talking off and on. I'm a little too old for her, and Lennon is a little too protective.

"I don't know if I truly believe you or not, but I'm gonna let it go, only because I agree. I can't be with her all the time. The fact of the matter is, she doesn't want me with her that much anymore. She's learning to live on her own, and I'd hate to take that independence away from her." She wipes under her eyes. "Just let her know I'm here if she needs me."

I'm an older sibling too. I know where she's coming from. It's hard to let the younger ones grow and not need you as much anymore. Walking over to her, I put my hands on her shoulders. "I promise. She's good. She's safe with me. No one is going to hurt her while I'm around, and while I wouldn't do this for anyone else, you can come out whenever you want to." This goes against everything I've thought since I moved out into my own place. I left the main house because I needed some time to myself after coming home. There were nights when I'd wake up in a cold sweat, sometimes screaming.

"Thank you, Devlin. I appreciate it."

Shrugging, I bend to grab the bags. "I gotta get back to the ranch, but if you need anything, let me know."

Leaving the law office, I grit my teeth. I've talked more in the past twenty-four hours than I have in the last couple of years.

"Hey, Devlin."

Turning, I raise my eyebrows at her. "Yeah?"

"If you ever need anything, let me know. I owe you for what you've done."

"Don't mention it." But in the back of my mind, I tuck the fact that she works for one of the best attorneys in South Dakota in my pocket. Who knows when I might need it.

FIVE
ATLEE

BEING ALONE in Devlin's space is different from what I imagined it would be. I always thought if I were given the chance, I'd be nosy and try to figure out all his secrets. Instead, I can't seem to make myself leave the bed. It smells like him, and I feel safer here than I have anywhere in my entire life.

Glancing around, I wonder what his plans were when he decided to move in here. Had he been planning to invite a woman? Was it done for one in particular? Was it always his plan to be alone and just invite women when he had an itch to scratch? All stuff I've thought about, but never been able to ask.

I'm not used to lying around all the time. Back when I lived at home with my parents, I would've gotten my ass beat had I decided to do that. So I make myself get out of bed and head to the bathroom. A shower is exactly what I need, but since I don't have any clothes to wear, I go back and forth on what I should do.

Worst comes to worst, I can get in Devlin's clothing and get at least a shirt and a pair of shorts.

When I get into the bathroom, I'm surprised. The house is little more than a cabin with one bedroom, a living area, and a kitchen, but the bathroom? This must be where Devlin spends most of his time. The bathtub is huge, a walk-in shower sits to the side with what looks like a steam option and a seat to relax on, and there's a hell of a view of the mountains from the picture window right above the tub.

This must be how Devlin relaxes after long days of hard work.

Searching around, I find some Epsom salt and start pouring a hot bath. It's exactly what I need to get rid of the soreness in my muscles. Once the large tub is full, I take off my clothes and sink down, more than enjoying the way the warm water encompasses my body and blocks out all the noise of the world around me.

I must doze off slightly, because I wake up with a start, my heart pounding when I hear a door open and shut. It takes me right back to the pharmacy, when I wasn't paying attention to who was coming or going. My hands shake as I put them over my breasts, trying to hide myself from whatever eyes are accompanying the footsteps heading toward the bathroom.

"Atlee, it's me."

Devlin's deep, dark voice brushes over me like a calming stroke on my back. Immediately, I feel safe again, like nothing is going to touch me while he's here. "In the bathroom. In the tub, actually."

He comes to the doorway, holding a bag in his hand. "Saw Lennon and grabbed this for you. She's worried about you."

"I know she is. It's her nature. You let her know I'm okay?"

He nods, grunting. "She knows. Does she believe it? That's another story."

I grin. He clocked her from a mile away. "Thank you for at least talking to her about it. That's half the battle. Now, why do you have such an amazing bathroom with this view? Do you spend a lot of time in here?"

He comes in, slow rolling those long legs and lean hips of his before setting the bag down and taking a seat on the edge of the tub. His hot gaze travels over my body, and it takes everything I have not to cover up. None of the boys my age have ever made me feel as seen as this man does. "The one thing I always wanted out in the field was a hot shower or a nice soak. So when I came home and decided to build this place, I knew what I wanted."

"And you got it?"

"And I got it."

There's something inherently attractive about a man who knows what he wants and goes for it. Tilting my head to the side, I can't help but flirt with him. I shouldn't, because I don't know where any of this is going, but I do, regardless of whether it's the right thing to do or not. "Do you always get what you want?"

The look he gives me is one of ownership as his gaze takes in my naked body. The tongue that made my knees weak last night licks his lips, and it takes everything I have for me not to come out of the water and attack him. I've never been what most would call in tune with my body. I've heard friends, my sister included, talking about how they've had fun with men, how they were wrecked by whomever they were dating. Before Devlin last night? I never had that. But I just did, and now I want more of it.

"Yeah," he answers. "I do usually get what I want."

I'm playing with fire. "Am I something you want?"

A groan fills the room as he drags a hand through his hair. The ink on his arm is captured by the light from the window. "Yeah." He pulls his bottom lip between his teeth. "Yeah, you're somethin' I want."

My eyes meet his, the heat flaring between the two of us. "What are you going to do about it?" I whisper, pulling my legs up in front of my chest.

He leans in, and my breath hitches. Having him this close, I can smell the woodsy scent that's his, coupled with the outdoors. "What I'd like to do is take these clothes off and slide in there next to you. That's what I'd love to do about it. Unfortunately, I have to go help Jesse and Truett move some cattle into the south field. I'll be back later. You gonna be here when I get here?"

This is the first time he's asked me about what I plan to do. "I'll be here. Hurry home, Devlin."

Curling a finger under my chin, he tips it up. "If you're waiting here for me? This'll be the quickest I've ever worked." With those words, he takes a kiss that sends heat through my body and dreams of the future through my head.

SIX
DEVLIN

I'M STILL HALF hard when I pull up to the barn at Grizzly River Ranch. Jesse and Truett are already there and watching as I put the truck in park and then hop out. "Why are y'all looking at me like I've grown a second head?"

Jesse gives me a grin. "Heard that Atlee's at your house. What the fuck? You never invite anyone over. Hell, I don't even know what the damn place looks like, and I'm your brother."

"Maybe because I like my privacy." I grab my hat from the passenger seat and put it on, adjusting it to block the morning sun. "Not all of us need an audience for everything we do."

"So why's Atlee there?" Truett asks, leaning against a fence post. His eyes are studying me like I'm a problem that needs solving. "Word travels fast around here. Heard there was trouble at the pharmacy."

I inhale deeply, trying to push away the anger that's been simmering since I found Atlee last night. "Some piece of shit roughed her up during a robbery. Beat her pretty bad." My jaw clenches at the memory. I'm ready to beat the shit out of someone again. "I got a call and went to get her."

Jesse straightens up, his expression hardening. "She okay?"

"Physically? She'll heal. Face is bruised, split lip. But she's tough." I walk past them toward the barn, not wanting to talk about the way my chest tightened when I saw her injured face, and how I wanted to keep the bastard for myself, instead of handing him over to the sheriff's department.

"Doesn't explain why she's at your place instead of her sister's or even hers," Jesse points out, following me. "You two got something going on I should know about?"

"Nothing for you to concern yourself with." I grab a saddle from the rack, hefting it over my shoulder. "She needed somewhere safe to stay, somewhere quiet. I offered."

Truett exchanges a look with Jesse. "You offered? Mr. Don't-Even-Come-Over-For-Christmas offered up his sacred bachelor pad?"

"She was scared, all right?" The words come out sharper than I intended. "You didn't see her face. Didn't see how she was shaking, trying to hold it together. I wasn't about to drop her off somewhere and leave."

Jesse raises his hands in surrender. "Easy, brother. Just surprised, is all. It's not like you to get involved in other people's problems."

"It's not like that." But even as I say it, I know it's a lie. Something about her pulls at me, makes me want to be closer. Makes me want things I haven't wanted in a long, damn time. Maybe even fucking forever.

"Sure, it's not." Jesse grabs his own saddle. "Keep lying to yourself."

"There's nothing going on." The memory of her lips against mine, the way she pressed her body into me, asking me to make her forget—it's burned into my mind like a brand.

"Whatever you say." Jesse's eyes narrow. "But I've never seen you move that fast for anyone outside family before."

"Can we just get to work?" I lead my horse out of the stall, throwing the saddle blanket over his back.

Truett comes up beside me, lowering his voice. "She really okay, though? That kind of thing can mess with someone's head."

I appreciate the genuine concern in his voice. Truett might give me shit like Jesse does, but he's been family since we were kids. "She's shaken up. Trying not to show it, but I can see it in her eyes. Just needs some time to feel safe again."

He nods, understanding. "And you're giving her that time. At your place. Where no one goes." The words drop in between us, a small smirk playing against his lips.

"Don't start."

"I'm just saying, for a man who values his solitude as much as you do, that's a big step."

I cinch the saddle tight, focusing on the task instead of Truett's knowing eyes. "She needed help. I helped. That's all there is to it."

"Sure." He doesn't sound convinced. "And when she's feeling better? When she doesn't need that help anymore?"

The question catches me off guard. I hadn't thought that far ahead. Last night was about getting her somewhere safe. Sleeping in the same bed, taking her mind off everything...well, something else entirely. I haven't considered what happens next.

"I'll cross that bridge when I come to it." I mount my horse, looking down at them both. "We moving this herd today, or are we just gonna stand around talking about my personal life all day?"

Jesse laughs as he finishes saddling his horse. "Just admit it, Dev. You like having her there."

I don't answer, but the truth is, I do. Waking up knowing she was in my house, seeing her in my bathroom, it felt right in a way I can't explain, even with the circumstances being what they are.

We ride out to the pasture in silence, the afternoon sun warming my back. It's a clear day, the kind that makes you appreciate living in open country. Up ahead, the cattle are scattered across the field, some grazing, others resting in the shade of the few trees.

"So," Jesse says as we spread out to begin gathering the herd. "Tell us what happened. How'd you end up being the one to save Atlee Walsh?"

I sigh, knowing they weren't about to let this go. "She called me. Said she was in trouble and needed help."

"She called you?" Truett asks, eyebrows raised. "Not 911? Not her sister?"

I shrug, trying to seem casual about it. "We've been...talking. Off and on."

"Talking?" Jesse's grin is wide enough to split his face. "Since when?"

"Since that night Truett got hurt, and she helped out. We've texted some. Talked when she's working at the diner." I guide my horse around a small group of calves, nudging them toward the others. "Nothing serious."

"Serious enough that you're the one she called when she was in trouble," Truett points out.

The memory flashes through my mind—her voice on the phone, small and frightened. The way my heart had stopped at the sound of it. How I'd dropped everything and raced to the pharmacy without a second thought.

"When I got there, things weren't good. Atlee was fighting for her life, looking like she'd gone ten rounds with a heavyweight." My grip tightens on the reins. "She didn't want to go to the hospital and didn't want her sister to see her like that."

"So you took her home with you," Jesse says, no longer teasing.

"What else was I supposed to do? Leave her there?"

"Could've taken her to Lennon's," Truett says. "Or brought her here so that Aubree could fuss over her. But you took her to your place." He stops so that the next words carry a ton of weight. "The one place none of us are allowed to go."

I don't have a good answer for that. It hadn't even occurred to me to take her anywhere else. From the moment I saw her, bruised and shaking, all I could think about was getting her somewhere I knew she'd be safe. Somewhere I could protect her.

We work in silence for a while, guiding the cattle toward the south pasture. It's familiar work, the kind that lets your mind wander. Mine keeps wandering back to Atlee, to the way she looked at me this morning, to the feel of her in my arms.

"You know," Jesse says as we reach the gate to the south pasture. "Having Atlee at your place, maybe it's not such a bad thing."

"What's that supposed to mean?"

He shrugs, guiding his horse alongside mine. "Just that maybe what you're missing in your life is a woman around. Someone to come home to."

"I'm not missing anything." The words come automatically, a defense I've used for years.

"Sure you are. We all need someone, Dev. Even you." He smiles, and it's not his usual shit-eating grin. It's softer. "Look at Aubree and me. I never thought I'd want someone around all the time until we stopped fighting each other. Now I can't imagine my life without her."

"That's you. I'm different."

"Are you? Or have you just convinced yourself of that because it's easier than taking a risk?" He opens the gate, letting the first of the cattle through. "All I'm saying is, now that she's there, you might find you don't want her to leave."

I don't respond, but his words settle in my chest like a stone. The thought of Atlee leaving, of my house going back to being empty and quiet—it doesn't sit right.

We spend the next few hours moving the rest of the herd, the rhythmic work giving me time to think. About Atlee. About what Jesse said. About the way I felt when I woke up this morning, knowing she was right there next to me.

When we finish, the sun is high overhead, beating down on us as we make our way back to the barn. I'm sweaty and tired, but my mind is clearer than it's been in a long time.

"Heading home?" Truett asks as we unsaddle our horses.

"Yeah. Want to check on Atlee." I don't bother hiding it now. They've already seen through me.

Jesse claps me on the shoulder. "Tell her I hope she feels better. And Dev?" He waits until I look at him. "It's okay to want something for yourself. It's okay to let someone in."

I nod, not trusting myself to speak. As I walk back to my truck, I can't help but wonder if Jesse isn't right. Maybe what's been missing from my life isn't just peace and quiet. Maybe it's been someone to share it with.

The thought of Atlee waiting for me at home makes my step a little lighter, my heart beating a little faster. For the first time in years, I find myself looking forward to something other than solitude.

SEVEN
ATLEE

THE SUN IS STARTING to set as I walk around Devlin's house. It's starting to get darker earlier, and soon it'll be getting cold. It probably won't even be much longer until we get the first snow. But what I've figured out today is that Devlin's house is cozy. There may not be a bunch of knickknacks everywhere, but there's a serenity that I've enjoyed.

My phone buzzes where it's sitting on the kitchen table. I reach over and grab it.

> **Lennon**
> Just checking on you. Everything going okay?

> **Me**
> Yeah, just waiting on Devlin to get here. He had to go to work earlier.

Lennon
Sounds really damn cozy, Atlee. Are you sure you know what the hell you're doing? He's as closed off as any other person I've ever seen when it comes to friendships or relationships.

I roll my eyes and have a seat on the couch, pulling my knees up to my chest.

Me
I appreciate you looking out for me, but he's different with me. Not as closed off...

Lennon
Isn't that what they all say?? You can fix them?

Bile rises up in my throat as I think about what she's saying. Those are famous last words. All women think they can fix the man they want to be with.

Me
There's nothing to fix. He lives his life the way he likes to live it. Really no different than me.

It's defensive, and I know it. It's exposing the fact that I've been infatuated with this man since I helped Truett.

Lennon
I get it. You've got a thing for him. Hell, I even understand it. He was nice when he came to get your bag, and he isn't hard on the eyes. I just want to make sure that you realize your heart is the one on the line here. You care about people fully and immediately. Are you sure that Devlin is the person you want to stake your heart on?

She's right to be asking. I had a bad experience when I was sixteen. I trusted a much older man that I never should have. Living with the parents we had will do that to you. You'll look at any man who gives you a little bit of attention as the man who can save you. I learned early, and that lesson has followed me.

Me
I'm okay, Len. I trust him. Maybe I shouldn't, but I do. I'm going into this with my eyes and heart wide open this time. I promise. I'm a big girl, and I can handle this.

Lennon
Okay, I love you. You know I'll be out there as soon as you let me know you need me, to come get you. I worry. I know you're an adult, I get it, but I'm always going to worry about you.

Me
I know.

When I hear a vehicle coming up the driveway, I look out, my stomach doing a flip when I see that it's Devlin.

Me
He's here, I'm going to talk to him, but if I need anyone, and I do mean anyone, you'll be the first one I call.

It's stupid how excited I am to see this man. I never saw myself as the type of woman who would go watch as her significant other came home from a long day at work. But here I am, getting up and walking out to the porch. It was dark when we came in last night, and I wasn't able to look around and see what the outside was like. Now, my gaze goes past where Devlin has parked his truck and to the main house at the ranch. Although it's several hundred feet from this house, I can imagine how grand it was back in its heyday. It's seen better days, judging by the peeling paint on the outside, but there are a few signs that it's being worked on.

In the backyard, there are brand new boards and what looks to be roofing material.

They're probably hoping to get it going before the first snow hits. Although it's warm during the day right now, it won't be long until it's really cold at night. Then, not long after, it'll be freezing.

But that's not happening right now, and my attention goes back to Devlin. I've never been the type of girl who thought she'd be with a man who wore a suit or a tie, but there wasn't a part of me who wondered if I'd be with a man who wore a pair of boots and a dirty flannel shirt either. For a long time, I thought I'd be by myself. Just like everything else, though, things can change.

Which is why I'm watching as Devlin gets out of his truck.

One dirty boot hits the dusty ground before the other. Jeans show his day of work in the dirt on the knees and thighs. His flannel sleeves are rolled up past his elbows, with his tattoos on display. It's all hot as fuck, and I find myself almost drooling as I watch his loose-legged stride head toward the house.

"You okay?" he barks out as he takes the steps two at a time.

"Yeah, yeah," I say as I push my hair back behind my ear. "I wanted to come out and see you. I heard your truck coming down the driveway."

"How'd you know it was me? It could've been someone else. Someone who was with the guy who robbed you at the pharmacy. Be careful, Atlee." His tone is sharp. I'm not prepared for it, so I flinch and close my eyes, counting to five. "Hell," he growls. "I'm sorry."

"Don't apologize." I hold up my hand. "You're right. I should've been more careful." Backing up, I hit the door. When I shrink into the doorway, he lifts his arm, putting his forearm above my head. Swallowing roughly, my eyes meet his, and that pull between us is there like it's been since the moment we met.

"You're right." He leans in. "You should be more careful, but maybe I should be less rough around the edges too."

I nod and then reach, looping my arms around his waist. "I missed you today." Those words come from my mouth before I can stop them. The truth is, I don't even mean to say them.

His body tenses for a split second before I feel his muscles relax under my touch. That broad chest of his rises with a deep breath, and his arm drops from above my head to wrap around my shoulders, pulling me closer.

"I missed you too," he admits, his voice low and rough, like it costs him everything to say those words. "Couldn't stop thinkin' about you while I was out there."

My heart jumps at his confession, and I can't help the smile that breaks across my face. I tilt my head back to look up at him, my chin resting against his chest.

"Yeah?" I question, enjoying the way his features soften just slightly when his eyes meet mine.

"Yeah," he confirms, the pad of his thumb brushing across my cheek. "Truett caught me staring off at nothing at least three times. Said I was distracted."

"Were you?" I can't help teasing him, standing on my tiptoes to get closer.

"What do you think?" His lips quirk into the hint of a smile. It transforms his whole face, making him look younger and less guarded. I want to see more of that.

"I think..." I trail off, pressing my body against his more firmly. "I think I like that I was on your mind."

He groans, dipping his head down until our foreheads touch. "You're trouble, Atlee."

"Good trouble, I hope."

"The best kind," he whispers, and then his mouth is on mine, hot and demanding. It's not the gentle kiss from this morning. This one is hungry, like he's been waiting all day to taste me again. His hand slides down to my lower back, pressing me against him as his tongue sweeps into my mouth.

I'm instantly lost in the sensation of him. My fingers dig into the solid muscle of his back, feeling the strength there as he holds me like I'm something precious. When we finally break apart, we're both breathing hard.

"Should we take this inside?" I ask, voice embarrassingly breathless.

He nods, his eyes dark with want, but then he takes a step back, giving us both some space. His hand finds mine, though, our fingers intertwining as he gently guides me back inside the house.

The warmth of the cabin envelops us as we step through the doorway. I watch as Devlin kicks off his boots by the door, revealing thick wool socks underneath. There's something oddly intimate about seeing him like this, the rugged cowboy transforming into someone more relaxed, more at home.

"Are you hungry?" I ask, looking toward the kitchen. "I could make us something to eat."

His eyebrow quirks up. "You cook?"

"Don't sound so surprised." I laugh. "I'm decent enough not to poison us both, at least."

That gets me another one of those rare smiles that makes my insides melt. "I'd like that," he says, running a hand through his hair. "Haven't had a home-cooked meal in this house that wasn't made by me in...hell, I don't think ever."

"Well then, I'm happy to change that." I head toward the kitchen, taking stock of what he has available. "I can throw together something simple with what you've got here."

He follows me, leaning against the doorframe, watching as I open cupboards and the refrigerator. "Need any help?"

"You can help by keeping me company," I tell him, pulling out pasta, canned tomatoes, and some dried herbs I spot in a rack. "And maybe by telling me how long you've been living out here alone."

He's quiet for a moment, and I wonder if I've pushed too far.

But then he moves to sit at the small kitchen table, stretching those long legs out in front of him.

"About five years," he finally answers. "Built this place myself."

"It's beautiful," I say honestly, filling a pot with water. "Especially that bathroom."

A chuckle rumbles from him. "Yeah, that was the priority."

I smile, setting the pot on the stove and turning to face him. "Can I ask you something?"

His face turns serious again, but he nods. "You can ask. Might not answer."

"Fair enough." I lean against the counter. "Will you tell me someday? About what made you want to be out here by yourself?"

Something flashes across his features—pain, maybe, or anger —but it's gone so quickly I can't be sure.

"Someday," he says quietly. "Not today."

I nod, accepting his answer. There's history there, and he's not ready to share it. That's okay. I have my own demons that I'm not ready to talk about either.

"You think you'll be able to go back to work on Monday?" he asks, clearly changing the subject.

I turn back to the stove, thinking about his question as I add salt to the now boiling water. The memory of the robbery flashes through my mind—the gun pointed at me, the fear that had paralyzed me. My hands start to shake slightly.

"I think so," I answer, trying to keep my voice steady. "I need to. Can't hide away forever, right? By then, I should be at least able to cover the bruises with makeup."

"No one would blame you if you needed more time," he says, and I can feel his eyes on my back.

"Maybe not," I acknowledge, adding the pasta to the water. "But I'd blame myself. I don't want to let fear win."

I hear the scrape of his chair, and then he's behind me, not touching, just close enough that I can feel his warmth.

"I'll take you," he says, his voice firm, not leaving room for argument. "I'll drive you there and pick you up when your shift is done."

I turn to face him, our bodies just inches apart. "You don't have to do that."

"I know I don't have to." His eyes hold mine, intense and determined. "I want to."

Warmth unfurls in my chest at his words. It's not just the offer of a ride. It's the promise of protection, of not having to face my fear alone. Maybe he won't make me go home by myself either. Living in my apartment, I always have an underlying feeling of anxiousness because I'm scared of someone taking advantage of me. Here, I can completely relax.

"Okay," I agree softly. "As long as you're with me, I think I'll be okay."

His hand comes up to cup my cheek, and I lean into his touch. "You're stronger than you think, Atlee. But yeah, I'll be with you."

The timer on my phone buzzes, breaking the moment. I turn back to the stove, stirring the pasta.

"You know," I say over my shoulder. "I've never cooked for a man before. Not like this."

"No?" There's curiosity in his voice.

"No. Never had anyone I wanted to cook for, I guess. Just

my sister." I start working on a simple sauce with the canned tomatoes, adding garlic and herbs.

"Well," he says, moving beside me to grab plates from the cupboard. "I'm honored to be the first."

I glance up at him, at this man who looks like he could wrestle a bear but who's setting his kitchen table with such care. "Want to help me finish this up?"

"Just tell me what to do," he says, rolling up his already rolled sleeves a little higher.

We work together, moving around each other in his small kitchen like we've done it a hundred times before. He chops some vegetables I found in his fridge while I finish the sauce, our elbows occasionally brushing, sending sparks across my skin each time.

"This smells amazing," he comments as I drain the pasta.

"Just wait until you taste it," I reply with a confidence I don't entirely feel. What if he hates it?

But when we sit down across from each other, and he takes his first bite, the appreciation on his face is unmistakable.

"Damn, Atlee," he says after swallowing. "Where'd you learn to cook like this?"

I shrug, pleased by his reaction. "Had to learn young. My parents weren't exactly the type to make sure dinner was on the table. Lennon took a job early, and it was up to me to make sure the other stuff was done. Make no mistake, she took care of me, and I took care of her."

His expression darkens slightly at the mention of my parents, but he doesn't push. Instead, he takes another bite, making a sound of satisfaction that sends heat rushing through me.

"Well, their loss is my gain," he says simply.

We eat in comfortable silence for a while, the day's exhaustion catching up to both of us. It's strange how natural this feels, sharing a meal with him in his home.

"Thank you," he says as he finishes his plate. "For cooking."

"Thank you for letting me stay here," I counter. "For keeping me safe."

His eyes meet mine across the table, serious and intent. "I'll always keep you safe, Atlee. As long as you want me to."

There's a promise in those words that makes my breath catch. We're dancing around something here, something bigger than just attraction or convenience.

"I should probably do these dishes," I say, not knowing how to respond to the intensity of the moment.

He stands, taking his plate to the sink. "We'll do them together."

And so we do, side by side at the sink, me washing while he dries. It's such a simple, domestic thing, but it feels significant somehow. Like we're building something, one small moment at a time.

When we're done, he takes my hand, his callused fingers wrapping around mine. "Come on," he says, leading me toward the living room. "Let's rest for a bit."

He sits on the couch and pulls me down beside him, his arm going around my shoulders as I curl against his side. Outside, the last light of day is fading, painting the mountains in shades of purple and blue.

"This is nice," I whisper, afraid to break the spell of contentment that's settled over us.

His fingers trace lazy patterns on my shoulder. "Yeah," he agrees, his voice a rumble I can feel through his chest. "It is."

I tilt my head up to look at him, finding his eyes already on me. There's a question there, one I'm not sure either of us is ready to answer yet. But for now, this is enough—his arms around me, the quiet of the evening, and the knowledge that whatever comes next, we'll face it together.

EIGHT
DEVLIN

I WASN'T EXPECTING Atlee to cook me dinner and wasn't expecting to enjoy it as much as I did. I've never met a woman who is as intriguing as she is. Although she's so much younger than I am, she seems to have the same type of life experience I do. She's wise beyond her years and compliments me more than anyone else ever has.

When I came home from the military, I came home to a shit show. I'd purposely ignored home after my parents died and left everything here for Jesse to deal with. It wasn't exactly my finest hour, and I had been so mad when I realized what he was doing to make sure the ranch stayed afloat.

At first, I was completely against the cattle rustling operation, and I wanted to go completely legit.

We'd argued, and he'd thrown my absence back in my face. It hadn't been the only thing that had been thrown back in my face, either. My high school girlfriend had moved on too, although we'd never actually broken up. But then again, I'd never made her a priority either.

The story of my life—letting everything fall to the wayside while I stay stuck in my own world.

Which is why I've decided to be more present, no matter how difficult it is in the grand scheme of things, and why I'm trying to be the man I believe Atlee deserves.

"I need a shower." I yawn as I stretch. "While it's nice lying here with you, tomorrow morning is going to come early. I have a TV in the bedroom. Wanna watch something after I take a shower?"

She nods, her eyes meeting mine. There's heat in her gaze. "Mind if I join you?"

We have to be careful. This relationship can't be built on the physical, but I want to be close to her like that, so I nod.

My throat goes dry as she stands up, stretching her arms above her head. The way her body moves makes my pulse quicken. I've been with women before, but never one who affects me like she does, who makes my skin feel too tight for my body with just a look.

"Lead the way," she says with a soft smile that's equal parts shy and bold, her eyes heating.

I push myself up off the couch, acutely aware of how small this cabin suddenly feels. When I first built it, it actually felt too big. Taking her hand, I guide her toward the bathroom, my mind racing with thoughts I shouldn't be having. She's been through hell, is still processing a traumatic experience, and here I am thinking about getting her naked.

But I'm not the one who suggested the shower, a voice in my head reminds me. She is.

Still, I need to be careful. This can't just be about physical release, not with her. Atlee deserves better than that, and I'm not entirely sure I'm capable of giving her what she needs.

When we reach the bathroom, I turn on the shower to let it heat up. Steam begins to fill the room as I turn back to face her. The way she's looking at me—like I'm her knight in shining armor, something worthy—makes my chest ache.

"You sure about this?" I ask, my voice rough, even to my own ears.

She steps closer, her fingers finding the buttons of her borrowed shirt—my shirt—and begins undoing them one by one. "I'm sure about you, Devlin."

Christ, she's going to be the death of me.

I watch, transfixed, as she reveals herself inch by inch. When the shirt falls open, exposing the curves of her breasts and the flat plane of her stomach, I have to clench my fists to keep from reaching for her.

"Your turn," she whispers, and there's vulnerability in her eyes that reminds me to take this slow, to be gentle.

I pull the T-shirt I wear under my flannel over my head, aware of her gaze traveling over my chest, lingering on the tattoos that map the story of my life across my skin. When her fingers trace the scar that runs along my ribs, a souvenir from a mission gone sideways in a place I'm still not allowed to talk about, I shiver.

"Does it hurt?" she asks.

"Not anymore."

We undress each other slowly, like we have all the time in the world. When we're both naked, I take a moment just to look at her, to commit every curve and line of her body to memory.

"You're beautiful," I tell her, because it's the truth and because some things need to be said out loud.

Color rises to her cheeks, but she doesn't look away. "So are you."

I lead her into the shower, the hot water cascading over us. For a moment, we just stand there, letting the warmth surround us, her back against my chest, my arms wrapped around her waist. I press my lips to her shoulder, tasting the water on her skin. My hand moves up, taking one of her breasts in my hands, and the other travels to curl around her neck, pulling the back of her head against my collarbone.

"This okay?" I murmur against her neck.

She turns in my arms, her hands sliding up my chest. "More than okay."

When she kisses me, it's different from before. It's slower, deeper, like she's trying to memorize the taste of me. I lose myself in the sensation of her mouth, her hands, her body pressed against mine under the steady stream of water.

I reach for the shampoo, pouring some into my palm. "Turn around," I tell her.

She does, and I work the shampoo into her long, dark hair, massaging her scalp with my fingertips. A soft moan escapes her lips, and the sound goes straight through me. I've never done this for anyone before. I never wanted to. But with Atlee, everything feels different. New.

After I rinse her hair, she returns the favor, her small hands working through my much shorter strands, nails scraping lightly against my scalp. It's such a simple thing, but it feels intimate in a way that catches me off guard.

When she reaches for the soap, I catch her wrist. "Atlee, we need to slow down."

Her brow furrows. "You don't want this? We've already done it before."

"That's not it." I cup her face with my hands, forcing myself to say what needs to be said. "I want you. More than I've wanted anything in a long damn time. But you've been through something traumatic, and I don't want to take advantage of that. Last night was about me making sure you were okay. Tonight would be me being selfish."

"You're not taking advantage," she argues, her wet hands coming to rest on my forearms. "I know what I want, Devlin."

"I believe you," I tell her, brushing my thumb across her cheekbone. "But I also know that sometimes, after something like what happened to you, you look for ways to feel safe, to feel in control again, and I don't want to be just that for you."

She's quiet for a moment, water droplets clinging to her eyelashes. "Is that what you think this is? Me using you because I'm scared?"

"No," I say quickly. "That's not what I meant. I just..." I struggle to find the right words. "I want to be sure that whatever happens between us is happening for the right reasons. For both of us."

Her expression softens, and she rises on her tiptoes to press a gentle kiss to my lips. "Okay," she whispers. "We'll take it slow from here on out."

Relief and disappointment war within me as I nod. "Thank you."

We finish our shower with gentle touches and soft kisses, nothing more. By the time we step out, the bathroom mirror is completely fogged over. I wrap her in a towel before securing one around my own waist.

"I'll get you something to sleep in," I tell her, heading to my dresser. I pull out an old T-shirt and a pair of drawstring shorts for her and a pair of sweatpants for myself. Although Lennon gave me her clothes, I really love the look of her in my stuff.

When she emerges from the bathroom wearing my clothes, her hair damp and clinging to her shoulders, something primal and possessive stirs in my chest. She looks right here, in my space, wearing my things.

"Which side of the bed do you prefer?" I ask, gesturing to the king-sized mattress that dominates my bedroom.

"I usually sleep on the right," she answers, hovering hesitantly at the edge of the room.

"Left side it is, then." I pull back the covers for her, watching as she slides between the sheets. After turning on the TV mounted on the wall opposite the bed, I join her, careful to leave a respectful distance between us.

She notices, of course. "I don't bite, you know," she teases, patting the space beside her. "Unless you want me to."

I can't help the laugh that escapes me. "You're dangerous, you know that?"

"So I've been told." She grins, and for a moment, all the shadows in her eyes are gone. "What are we watching?"

I hand her the remote. "Your choice."

She scrolls through the options, stopping when she sees a familiar title. "Oh! *Friday Night Lights*. Have you seen it?"

"Have I seen it?" I raise an eyebrow. "Clear eyes, full hearts..."

"Can't lose," she finishes with me, her smile widening. "No way. You're a fan too?"

"One of the best shows ever made," I confirm, settling back against the pillows. "Used to watch it overseas whenever I could. Something about it just...helped, you know? Reminded me of home, even when I was trying to forget."

"My comfort show too," she admits, selecting an episode from season one. "I used to hide in my room and watch it when things got bad at home. It made me believe that somewhere people actually cared about each other like that."

The casual way she references her childhood hits me in the gut. I know enough about the Walsh family to understand that her upbringing was far from ideal, but hearing her talk about it so matter-of-factly makes me want to hunt down everyone who ever hurt her.

"Come here," I say, holding out my arm.

She scoots over, nestling against my side like she belongs there. I pull the blanket up over us both as the familiar theme song plays.

"I always wanted to be like Coach Taylor," I admit, absently stroking her hair. "The way he led, you know? Firm but fair. Demanded excellence but showed compassion too. It's what I imagined life would be like when I came home."

"Mmm," she hums against my chest. "I could see that. You've got that whole strong, silent type thing going."

"That so?"

"Definitely. And Tami Taylor was my role model," she says. "Strong, smart, didn't take crap from anyone, but had the biggest heart. I wanted to be like that."

"You are," I tell her, and I mean it. "Strong as hell, but kind too."

She tilts her head up to look at me, surprise in her eyes. "You think?"

"I know."

We watch in comfortable silence for a while, her body warm against mine. Occasionally, one of us comments on a scene or quotes a line just before the character says it, making the other laugh. It feels...normal. Comfortable. Like we've been doing this forever instead of just one night.

As the episode ends, she yawns, her eyelids growing heavy. "One more?" she asks sleepily.

"One more," I agree, though I doubt she'll make it through. Sure enough, halfway through the next episode, her breathing deepens and evens out, her body going slack against mine.

I look down at her sleeping face, all the tension gone from her features. She looks younger in sleep, more vulnerable, and the need to protect her swells in my chest until it's almost painful.

Carefully, I reach for the remote and turn off the TV, plunging the room into darkness except for the soft moonlight filtering through the curtains. I should probably move her, give her space to sleep comfortably, but I can't bring myself to disturb her. Instead, I adjust my position slightly, settling in with her head on my chest, my arm around her shoulders.

This wasn't how I expected my night to go when I drove home from work. Hell, this wasn't how I expected any part of my life to go. I came back to Grizzly River to make amends, to help Jesse, to try to figure out what the hell I was supposed to do with the rest of my life now that the military was behind me.

I never expected Atlee Walsh to crash into my carefully ordered existence, turning everything upside down.

Yet, as I lie here with her breathing softly against me, her hand curled trustingly over my heart, I realize something that scares the shit out of me. If someone asked me right now what my perfect life looks like, it's this. It's her in my arms, in my home, in my life. It's shared showers, home-cooked meals, and watching our favorite shows together. It's the easy conversation and the comfortable silences.

It's having someone who sees the darkness in me and isn't afraid of it. Someone who's got her own shadows but lets me see them too.

The realization should send me running. It's too fast, too intense, too everything. But instead, I find myself tightening my arm around her, pressing a kiss to the top of her head.

"Sweet dreams, Atlee," I whisper into the darkness, knowing she can't hear me but needing to say it anyway.

As I drift off to sleep, I wonder if maybe, just maybe, I've finally found something worth staying for. Something worth fighting for.

And if that something is the woman in my arms, I'm pretty damn lucky.

NINE
ATLEE

THE WEEKEND WENT by much faster than I thought it would. When Devlin wasn't doing weekend chores at the ranch, he was in his cabin with me. When my alarm went off, I wasn't prepared, which is why I'm now staring at myself in the mirror, hyping myself up so that I can get ready to go to work.

The bruises have faded, and I'm trying to figure out if I can hide most of them with the makeup I have.

"Are you nervous?" Devlin asks as he comes into the bathroom. He's wearing a white T-shirt and an unbuttoned pair of jeans. The ink on his arms is highlighted by the shocking brightness of his shirt, and I can't help but reach out and run my fingernails along his skin.

"Yeah," I admit, my voice small and quiet. "I'm dreading walking in there."

"There will be a lot of fuckin' feelings," he grunts as he reaches out and wraps his arms around my waist, propping his chin on my shoulder.

The picture we make in the mirror is one I hope I never forget. Even if whatever this is doesn't last, I'll have these memories. "There will. I'm scared that I won't be able to stay. That I'll walk in and immediately freak out before running through the front door. What if I'm not strong enough for this?"

"You're strong enough for it," he whispers in my ear. "You're one of the strongest people I know, and if you can't do it? I'll have the getaway car outside for you."

I smile, and he answers the gesture in the mirror. "I do have a serious question for you, Devlin."

"What, babe?"

He's never called me anything like that before, and the warmth that spreads across my face and chest is visible by the blush that takes over my flesh. "I don't know how to say this..."

"Just say it. I think you know you can tell me anything at this point."

He's right. We've moved far enough along in our relationship that I shouldn't hide things, no matter if they're hard to put voice to. "What if I'm not ready to stay in my apartment by myself?" I say the words quickly, without taking a breath.

"Then you come here," he answers matter-of-factly. "You stay here for as long as you want. Do you have a car?" he asks, as if this is the first time he's thought of it.

"I have one, but it's broken down. I live close enough to the pharmacy that I can walk. So it's like..." I wring my hands together. "I've lost that safety too. I'm not sure I feel safe enough to walk back and forth now."

He reaches forward, grabbing my chin, tilting my face up so that our eyes meet in the mirror again. "I'll take you until we can get you a vehicle out here. It'll take me a couple of days, but you can stay here for as long as you want to."

"I didn't tell you all this so you would feel the need to fix everything for me," I argue.

He grunts. "Fixing is what I do for the people I care about. Let me do this."

For so long, no one cared other than Lennon. It's foreign for someone other than her or me to care about my safety and to make sure I have everything I need. The people who should've been the ones to do that? They never did, and now this big, amazing man wants to be the one to do it. "Okay," I agree. "I'll let you help me. For some reason, I feel like I'm supposed to."

"You're in this position because you're meant to be here?" he questions.

"Yeah, that's exactly it."

He pulls me back against his chest. "Then I'm glad we both feel the same way."

I take one final look at myself in the mirror, checking the concealer I've applied over the worst of the bruising. It's not perfect, but it's the best I can do. The dark purple has faded to a sickly yellowish-green around my eye, and my split lip is mostly healed. I look like I've been through something, but I don't look broken. That's what matters.

"You ready?" Devlin asks from the doorway, keys in hand. He's fully dressed now, with jeans buttoned, boots on, and a flannel shirt over his white tee. He looks good. So damn good that for a second I consider asking him to take me back to bed instead of to work. Ignoring my responsibilities is so tempting.

"As ready as I'll ever be," I reply, grabbing my bag. "Let's go before I change my mind."

Outside, the morning is crisp, the kind of early autumn day that makes you want to curl up with a blanket and a hot drink. Instead, I'm climbing into Devlin's truck, my heart racing at the thought of returning to the place where I was assaulted.

Devlin starts the engine but doesn't put the truck in drive right away. Instead, he turns to me, his expression serious. "Remember, you don't have to do this today. You can call in, take more time."

I shake my head. "No, I need to go back. The longer I wait, the harder it'll be."

He studies my face for a moment, then nods, satisfied that I mean what I say. "All right then. Let's go."

As we drive down the winding road from his cabin toward town, I stare out the window, watching the trees and pastures roll by. Devlin reaches over and takes my hand, his much larger one engulfing mine. He doesn't speak, just holds on, his thumb tracing small circles against my skin. It's a small gesture, but it grounds me, reminding me I'm not alone in this.

"Tell me something I don't know about you," I say suddenly, needing the distraction.

He raises an eyebrow. "Like what?"

"Anything. Something nobody else knows."

He's quiet for a long moment, thinking. "I used to be afraid of horses," he finally says, his voice low.

I turn to him, surprised. A giggle works its way past my lips. "What? You? But you work with them every day."

"Exactly why nobody knows," he says with a small smile. "When I was really young, I fell off one of the ranch horses. Got the wind knocked out of me. I was scared to get back on for months."

"What changed?"

"Jesse," he says simply. "He didn't know I was scared, just thought I was being lazy, avoiding chores. Called me a coward. Even back then, we were assholes to each other. My younger brother has always been my biggest competitor and the person to push me to do all the things I need to." His jaw tightens. "So I got back on the next day."

"And you weren't scared anymore?"

"Oh, I was terrified," he admits, his fingers tightening around mine. "But I was more afraid of my brother thinking I was weak. After a while, it got easier. Now I can't imagine not working with them."

I understand what he's not saying—that sometimes you have to face what scares you, even when every instinct tells you to run. It's what I'm doing today.

"Your turn," he says, glancing at me. "Tell me something I don't know about you."

I think about it, trying to find something that feels right to share. "I used to dream about owning a coffee shop," I say finally. "Not just working in one, but having my own place. With a little bakery inside and big comfy chairs where people could sit and read."

"Why didn't you?"

I shrug. "Life, I guess. My parents weren't exactly supportive of dreams. And then I needed to pay bills, so I took the pharmacy job because it paid better. I got a scholarship to get my pharmacy tech license, so it was easier for me to take that opportunity. And now..." I trail off.

"And now?" he prompts.

"I don't know. Maybe someday." I look out the window

again, watching as we get closer to town. "Do you think it's stupid? The coffee shop idea?"

"No," he says firmly. "I don't think any dream that lights you up like that is stupid."

We fall into silence as we approach Murphy's General Store, where the pharmacy is located. My stomach clenches at the sight of the familiar storefront, and my hand tightens around Devlin's involuntarily.

"Hey," he says softly. "Look."

I follow his gaze and feel a rush of emotion as I spot Lennon standing by the entrance. She's not alone. Payton, my coworker, is there too, along with Joseph, my boss. They're all waiting. For me.

"They came," I whisper, blinking back sudden tears, my throat tight.

"Of course they did," Devlin says, like it's the most obvious thing in the world. He pulls the truck into a parking space and turns to me. "You've got a lot of people in your corner, Atlee. More than you realize."

He gets out and comes around to my side, opening my door. I sit there for a moment, frozen, until he holds out his hand. "I've got you," he says.

I take his hand and let him help me down from the truck. My legs feel shaky, but I make myself put one foot in front of the other as we walk toward the entrance where my sister and colleagues are waiting.

Lennon rushes forward, wrapping me in a hug that's just this side of too tight. "You're really doing this?" she whispers in my ear.

"I'm really doing this," I confirm, hugging her back just as fiercely.

She pulls back, examining my face. "You look good. Better than I expected."

"Thanks to him," I say, nodding toward Devlin, who's hanging back, giving us space.

Payton steps forward next, her usual energetic self. "We cleaned everything up," she tells me, her voice softer than normal. "And Joseph rearranged some of the shelving, so it...it doesn't look the same as before."

I swallow hard, touched by the thoughtfulness. "Thank you."

Joseph, who's been my boss since I started and has never once shown much emotion, clears his throat. "We're glad to have you back, Atlee. Take it easy today, all right? Short shifts this week."

"I will," I promise.

The four of them—Lennon, Payton, Joseph, and Devlin—form a loose circle around me, and I realize what they're doing. They're creating a buffer, making it easier for me to walk through those doors again. My throat tightens with emotion.

"Ready?" Joseph asks.

I nod, and we move forward as a group. As we reach the door, Devlin hangs back. I turn to him, questioning.

"I'll be here to pick you up when your shift ends," he says, his eyes holding mine. "You've got this," he repeats his words from earlier.

"Thank you," I say, wishing I had better words to express what I'm feeling. But he seems to understand, nodding once before stepping back.

As I turn to enter the store, I catch sight of Deputy Noah Sanchez across the street. He's not looking at me, though. His gaze is fixed on Devlin, watching intently as he gets back in his truck. There's something in his expression that makes me uneasy. I make a mental note to tell Devlin about it later.

The bell above the door chimes as we enter, and I flinch at the sound, memories of that day threatening to overwhelm me. But Lennon's hand is steady on my back, Payton is chattering about the new inventory that came in, and Joseph is leading the way toward the pharmacy counter. I take a deep breath and follow them, my feet remembering the path even as my mind races with anxiety.

The pharmacy section has been rearranged, just as Payton said. The counter where I was standing when the robbery happened has been moved, and the display that was knocked over has been replaced with something entirely different. It's still the same place, but different enough that I don't immediately flash back to that moment.

"We thought it might help," Joseph says quietly, noticing my reaction. "Give you a fresh start."

"It does help," I assure him, running my hand along the new counter. "Thank you."

Lennon stays for another ten minutes, fussing over me until I finally convince her that I'm okay to work my shift. "I'll call you on my break," I promise her. "And Devlin is picking me up afterward."

She eyes me knowingly. "Things are getting serious there, huh?"

"I don't know what they are," I admit. "But they're something."

"Just be careful with your heart," she says, squeezing my hand. "And call me if you need anything."

After she leaves, Payton shows me the changes they've made to the workflow while I was gone, and Joseph goes over the reduced schedule he's created for me this week. By the time the store opens for customers, I'm feeling almost normal, focused on the familiar routine of my job.

The first customer through the door is Mrs. Henderson, an elderly woman who comes in every first Monday of the month for her blood pressure medication. She takes one look at me, and her eyes widen.

"Oh, Atlee, honey," she says, reaching across the counter to pat my hand. "I heard what happened. Are you all right?"

I paste on my best professional smile, the one I've perfected over years of lying about my family life. "I'm doing much better. Thank you for asking."

"Well, we've all been praying for you," she tells me earnestly. "The whole town was just sick about it. That man's not from around here, you know. Some drifter passing through."

I nod, not trusting myself to speak. The thought that everyone in town knows what happened to me, and has been discussing it, makes my skin crawl. But I shouldn't be surprised. News travels fast in Grizzly River.

"Anyway," Mrs. Henderson continues. "It's good to see you back at work. Shows real character."

"Thank you," I say, turning to retrieve her prescription. "How have you been feeling? Any dizziness with the new medication?"

And just like that, we slip into the familiar rhythm of pharmacist and patient, the conversation steering away from my trauma and back to her health. I can do this, I realize. I can pretend everything is normal, even when it isn't.

As the morning progresses, more customers come in. Some are awkward, avoiding eye contact or the subject altogether. Others are like Mrs. Henderson, full of concern and questions. A few pretend nothing happened at all, which I find I prefer. Each interaction gets a little easier, my shoulders gradually relaxing as I fall back into the routine of my job.

During a quiet moment, Payton brings me a cup of coffee from the café section of the store. "You're doing great," she tells me, bumping her shoulder against mine. "Seriously. I don't know if I could have come back so soon."

I wrap my hands around the warm cup. "I almost didn't," I admit. "If it weren't for Devlin..." I trail off, not sure how to explain what he's done for me, how he's made me feel safe enough to face this.

"He seems intense," Payton says, watching me carefully. "In a good way, I mean. Like, he'd move mountains for you if he had to."

I smile, thinking about how accurately that describes him. "Yeah, I think he would."

"So that's a thing now?" she asks, eyes dancing with curiosity. "You and the big, scary rancher?"

"It's...something," I say, echoing what I told Lennon. "I'm not sure what yet."

"Well, whatever it is, it looks good on you," she says with a wink. "Even with the bruises."

The rest of the morning passes without incident. I help customers, fill prescriptions, check inventory—all the normal tasks that used to fill my days before everything changed. There are moments when the anxiety spikes, like when a man in a dark hoodie walks in—it turns out he just has a cold and needs a decongestant. Or when I hear a loud crash from the grocery section—just a display of canned soup knocked over by a child. Each time, I breathe through it, reminding myself that I'm safe, that what happened was an isolated incident.

By the time my shortened shift is ending, I'm exhausted but proud. I made it through. I didn't run. I didn't break down. I just did my job, one minute at a time, until the hours had passed.

As I'm gathering my things to leave, I glance out the front windows and see Devlin's truck pulling up. Right on time, just like he promised. Something warm unfurls in my chest at the sight of him, this man who's become my safe harbor in such a short time.

"Your ride's here," Payton says with a knowing grin. "Same time tomorrow?"

"Same time tomorrow," I confirm, surprising myself with how much I mean it. Today was hard, but I did it. Tomorrow will be a little easier, and the day after that, even more so.

As I walk toward the exit, Joseph calls my name. "Atlee, wait." He comes over, awkward in the way he always is when dealing with anything personal. "You did good today. Real good."

"Thank you," I say, touched by the rare praise.

"And, uh...take care getting home, all right?" he adds, his eyes darting to where Devlin waits in his truck. There's something in his expression I can't quite read.

"I will," I assure him, before pushing through the door into the late afternoon sunlight.

As I walk toward Devlin's truck, I feel lighter than I have in days. I didn't let fear win today. I faced it head-on and came out on the other side. Now I'm going home, not to my empty apartment, but to a cabin in the mountains with a man who makes me feel safe and seen.

Not a bad way to end the day, all things considered.

TEN
DEVLIN

I PARK NEXT to the curb and go to get out of my truck, but Atlee comes running out before I can. She opens the passenger-side door and hops up. "Hey." I reach over, grabbing her chin and pulling her gaze to mine. "You doing okay?"

"Yeah." She smiles. "Today was a lot better than I expected it to be."

The anxiety I've been feeling since I dropped her off lessens. The tightness in my chest eases. "Good, I'm really glad to hear that. My brother and Aubree invited us over to the big house for dinner tonight. Are you feeling up to it? It'll just be us four. I told them if you weren't, we wouldn't do it."

My gaze follows her hands as she runs her palms up and down her scrub-covered thighs. "That would be fun. I know Aubree, not as well as Lennon does, but I like her. She's always been an amazing friend to Lennon, and in turn, to me. Maybe it's time we stop keeping ourselves hidden from everyone else?"

"I don't know." I give her a grin. "I like keeping you to myself."

She grins back at me. "Yeah, but it's probably not completely healthy mentally."

While she's not wrong, I still just want the two of us to be with one another. I've never been so obsessed with someone. I thought about her all day today while I was working, wondering how she was doing. I even texted her, but because of where we were, the text didn't go through, which is probably for the best. "Probably not, but we only have to answer to ourselves, right?"

"True. Thank you for today, Devlin. Hell, thank you for everything."

Did she think I'd be anywhere else? "There's no other place I'd rather fuckin' be, Atlee. For some reason, the two of us met each other, and you were pushed into my life. I'm not about to let shit go just because it got hard. That's not who I am."

"And thank God for that."

I put the truck in drive and pull away from the curb, stealing glances at her as she settles into the passenger seat. Relief washes over me seeing her so relaxed. All day, my mind had been creating worst-case scenarios—her breaking down, having a panic attack, or worse, the guy who'd hurt her somehow showing up.

"So how was it really?" I ask, keeping my voice casual. "And don't bullshit me. I want to know."

She sighs, looking out the window. "It was hard at first. Walking through that door...I thought I might throw up. But everyone was so kind. Joseph rearranged the whole pharmacy section so it wouldn't look the same, and Payton kept things light, which helped."

"And the customers?"

"Some were awkward. Most were nice. A few pretended nothing happened, which was actually kind of a relief." She turns to look at me, those blue eyes of hers catching the late afternoon light. "Oh, and I saw Deputy Noah Sanchez watching you this morning when you dropped me off."

My hands tighten on the steering wheel. "Watching me?"

"Yeah, he was across the street. Didn't even look at me, just had his eyes on you the entire time. It was weird."

Shit. That's not good. Noah has been poking around the ranch lately, asking too many questions. I keep my face neutral, not wanting to worry her. "Probably nothing. He's always been nosy."

"Maybe," she says, but I can tell she's not convinced. "Anyway, I just thought you should know."

"Thanks," I say, reaching over to take her hand. "I appreciate you looking out for me."

She squeezes my fingers. "Well, it goes both ways, right?"

"Right." I bring her hand to my lips, pressing a kiss against her knuckles. "Always."

As we drive toward the ranch, she tells me more about her day. I listen, asking questions when appropriate, but mostly just letting her talk. She seems lighter with each mile we cover, the tension easing from her shoulders.

"So...this dinner," she says as we turn onto the long driveway that leads to the main house. "Will it be formal? I'm still in my work clothes."

I glance at her scrubs. "You're fine. It's just Jesse and Aubree. Besides, nothing at the ranch is ever formal. We're lucky if Jesse remembers to take his boots off before coming in the house."

That gets a laugh out of her, which was my goal. The sound of it warms something inside me. I've never been the type of man who needs to make a woman laugh, but with Atlee, I find myself wanting to hear that sound as often as possible.

The main house comes into view, a large two-story structure that's seen better days. Parts of the exterior are being renovated, with new boards replacing rotted ones and fresh paint covering the peeling old layer. It's a work in progress, much like everything else at Grizzly River Ranch.

"I forget how beautiful this place is," Atlee murmurs, taking in the sprawling property. "Even with all the work it needs."

"It'll get there," I tell her. "Truett and Aubree are determined to restore it to its former glory. Just takes time and money, neither of which we have in abundance."

I park near the front porch, cutting the engine. Before I can come around to her side, Atlee is already out of the truck, stretching her arms above her head. The movement pulls her scrub top up slightly, revealing a sliver of skin at her waist. My mouth goes dry at the sight.

"You ready?" I ask, my voice rougher than I intended.

She nods, dropping her arms. "Lead the way, cowboy."

We don't even make it to the front door before it swings open, revealing Aubree with her blonde hair pulled back in a ponytail, wearing jeans and a flannel that probably belongs to my brother.

"You made it!" she exclaims, stepping forward to envelop Atlee in a hug. "I'm so glad you could come."

Atlee returns the hug, a genuine smile crossing her face. "Thanks for having us."

Aubree pulls back, looking Atlee over with a critical eye. "You look good. How was today?"

"It was okay," Atlee says simply. "Better than expected."

Aubree seems to understand not to push for more details. Instead, she links her arm through Atlee's. "Well, you're in for a treat tonight. Cookie heard you were coming for dinner and insisted on making something special."

I follow them inside, immediately hit with the smell of fried chicken and fresh-baked bread. My stomach growls in response. I'd been too distracted to eat lunch, worried about how Atlee was faring at work.

"Cookie made this just for me?" Atlee asks, sounding surprised as we enter the kitchen.

"Sure did," Aubree confirms. "Said every girl deserves her favorite meal after a hard day. Hope you like fried chicken, mashed potatoes and gravy, green beans, and cornbread."

Atlee's eyes widen. "That's...that's actually my favorite. How did he know?"

"Cookie knows everything," I say, placing my hand on the small of her back. "It's a little unnerving sometimes."

"It's because I listen," comes a gruff voice from the pantry. Cookie emerges, a stout man in his sixties with a perpetually flour-dusted apron. He's been with the ranch since before I was born. "Something most men could stand to learn."

He gives Atlee a once-over, then nods approvingly. "You look like you could use a good meal, young lady. Dinner'll be ready in ten."

With that, he disappears back into his domain, leaving Atlee looking both touched and slightly bewildered.

"Don't mind him," Aubree says with a laugh. "He acts gruff, but he's got the biggest heart. Come on. Jesse's in the dining room, setting the table. Or at least he better be, if he knows what's good for him."

We follow Aubree through to the dining room, where my brother is indeed placing silverware at each setting. He looks up as we enter, his face breaking into a rare smile when he sees Atlee.

"Well, look who it is," he says, coming around the table to give her a quick, somewhat awkward hug. Jesse has never been big on physical affection. "Heard you went back to work today. That takes guts."

"Thanks," Atlee says, seeming a bit surprised by the warmth of his greeting. "It wasn't easy, but it had to be done."

"Still, it takes a lot of guts and strength. If anyone knows, it's us," he says with a nod. "Sit, sit. Cookie's been fussing over this meal all afternoon."

We take our seats around the old oak table that's been in our family for generations. It's scarred and worn, but solid, a bit like the ranch itself. I notice that Aubree has added fresh wildflowers in a mason jar as a centerpiece, a touch that makes the room feel more welcoming.

"Beer?" Jesse offers, already heading toward the fridge.

"Please," I say, while Atlee nods her agreement.

He returns with four bottles, passing them around before taking his seat beside Aubree.

"So," Jesse says, clearly steering the conversation away from Atlee's first day back at work. "I was thinking we should show you around the property sometime, Atlee. Devlin says you've never seen the whole ranch."

"I'd like that," she replies, taking a sip of her beer. "I've only ever seen it from the road. I've never seen all of Grizzly River or Dark Skies. At some point, I'd love to see both, but no pressure."

"It's beautiful in the fall," Aubree adds. "The aspen trees turn this amazing gold color, especially up by the north pasture."

The conversation flows easily from there, with Jesse and Aubree taking turns telling stories about the ranch's history and their plans for its future. I'm grateful for the way they're including Atlee, making her feel welcome without putting her on the spot about recent events.

"We're hoping to have the barn renovation completed before winter sets in," Jesse explains, gesturing with his beer. "It's been a long time coming."

"The original structure dates back to the 1800s," I add, mostly for Atlee's benefit.

"That's amazing," Atlee says, genuine interest in her voice. "So the ranch has been in your family all this time?" she asks Aubree.

Aubree nods. "It hasn't always been easy, but it's home," she finishes. "You'll learn a lot about it if you stick around."

Cookie brings in the food then, placing heaping platters and bowls in the center of the table. The fried chicken is golden brown and crispy, the mashed potatoes creamy and flecked with black pepper, the gravy rich and thick. The green beans are cooked with pieces of bacon, and the cornbread comes in individual squares, steam rising from their tops.

"This looks incredible," Atlee says, her eyes wide.

Cookie gives a grunt that might be his version of a thank you before disappearing back to the kitchen.

We dig in, the conversation pausing as we all enjoy the meal. I watch Atlee take her first bite of chicken. The way her eyes close in appreciation, I feel a surge of something warm in my chest. She fits here, I realize, with my family, in this house. The thought should terrify me, but instead, it feels right.

"Oh, Devlin," Aubree says suddenly, breaking the comfortable silence. "I meant to tell you earlier. I saw Deputy Noah Sanchez this morning when I was getting coffee at Murphy's. He was watching you pretty intently when you left after dropping Atlee off."

So not only did Atlee see it, but Aubree did too. I freeze midbite, my eyes meeting Jesse's across the table. A silent communication passes between us. We need to talk, but not in front of the women.

"That right?" I say, keeping my tone casual. "Guess I'm just that good looking."

Aubree rolls her eyes. "I'm serious. It was weird. Like he was waiting for you specifically."

"Noah's always had a stick up his ass about the Nelsons," Jesse says, his voice light but his eyes hard. "Ever since high school, when Devlin here stole his girlfriend."

"I didn't steal anyone," I protest, grateful for the deflection. "She wasn't happy with him, so she moved on. Not my fault I was the better option." I don't mention that she's the high school girlfriend I assumed would've waited for me while I was off fighting for our country.

Atlee raises an eyebrow at me. "Somehow I'm not surprised you were a heartbreaker even then."

The tension eases as everyone laughs, and the conversation shifts to safer topics. But I can tell from the set of Jesse's shoulders that he's as concerned as I am about Noah's interest in our comings and goings.

After dinner, when the plates are cleared and dessert has been served, Jesse stands, stretching.

"Devlin, why don't you join me on the porch for a bourbon? The ladies can catch up."

It's not really a question, and Atlee seems to sense it. She gives my hand a squeeze under the table. "Go ahead. Aubree and I have plenty to talk about."

The night air is cool, a hint of the coming winter in its bite. Jesse retrieves a bottle of bourbon and two glasses from a cabinet near the door, pouring us each a generous measure before handing me one.

"Noah," he says simply, leaning against the porch railing.

"Yeah," I agree, taking a sip of the amber liquid, feeling it burn its way down my throat. "He's getting bolder."

"You think he knows? About the cattle?"

I consider the question carefully. We were careful about the rustling up until a few weeks ago. We made the decision to go legit, but it doesn't take away all the shit we did before then. Noah has always been more observant than the average deputy, and he did see us the night everything went to hell.

"I don't know," I admit. "But he's suspicious, and that's bad enough."

Jesse runs a hand through his hair, a gesture I recognize from our childhood. He's worried. "We need to be careful what we say around others."

"Agreed." I take another sip of bourbon. "And if he

approaches any of us, we need a plan. Lennon, Atlee's sister, works for Shawn Cooper. She offered legal help if we ever need it."

Jesse's eyebrows shoot up. "She offered? Just like that?"

"Says she owes me for helping Atlee." I shrug. "I'm not planning on cashing in that chip unless it's absolutely necessary, but it's good to have options."

"If Noah approaches any of us, we call Lennon and request the lawyer," Jesse says decisively. "No exceptions. We don't say a word without representation."

"Agreed," I say again, raising my glass in a mock toast. "Here's to staying one step ahead of the law."

Jesse clinks his glass against mine, but his expression remains serious. "I'm worried about you, Dev."

"Me? Why?"

"Because you've got more to lose now," he says, nodding toward the house where Atlee sits. "You care about her. That makes you vulnerable."

I can't deny it, so I don't try. "Yeah, I do care about her. But that doesn't change anything. I mean, you have a shit ton to lose too, motherfucker, unless you don't think Aubree could be in trouble too?"

"Doesn't it?" Jesse challenges. "Can you honestly tell me you're comfortable bringing her into this life? With all its risks?"

The question hits a nerve. I've been avoiding thinking about it—about how my feelings for Atlee complicate things, about how I'm putting her in danger just by association if Noah ever finds concrete evidence against us.

"I don't know," I admit, the words difficult to say. "But I'm not willing to let her go either."

Jesse studies me for a long moment, then nods. "Then we'll just have to be extra careful. For her sake as well as ours."

We finish our drinks in silence, each lost in our own thoughts. The night has deepened around us, stars appearing one by one in the vast Dakota sky. Finally, I push away from the railing.

"I should get her home. She's had a long day."

Jesse claps a hand on my shoulder. "It's good to see you... happy."

The word sounds strange applied to me, but I can't deny it's accurate. Despite the complications, despite the dangers, I am happy with Atlee in a way I've never been before.

Back inside, we find the women laughing over some shared joke. Atlee's face is flushed with amusement, her eyes bright, and the sight of her like this, relaxed and unguarded, makes something tighten in my chest.

"Ready to head out?" I ask, coming to stand beside her chair.

She looks up at me, still smiling. "Whenever you are."

We say our goodbyes, with promises to do this again soon. Aubree hugs Atlee, whispering something in her ear that makes her laugh. Jesse gives her a more reserved farewell, but I can tell he's warming to her.

In the truck, driving back to my cabin, Atlee leans her head against the window, looking tired but content. "That was nice," she says softly. "Jesse and Aubree are cute together."

"They liked you," I tell her, reaching over to take her hand. "Not that I'm surprised."

"What did you and Jesse talk about out there? Noah?"

She's perceptive, this woman of mine. "Among other things,"

I admit, not wanting to lie to her but not wanting to burden her with the full truth either. "Just being cautious."

She nods, accepting this. "I get the feeling there's a story there, but I won't push. Just know that I'm here if you ever want to talk about it."

"I know," I say, squeezing her hand. "Thank you."

When we reach the cabin, I drive around to the back instead of parking in my usual spot out front. Atlee gives me a questioning look, but I just smile.

"I have something to show you."

As I turn off the engine, her eyes widen at the sight of two rocking chairs sitting side by side on the back porch, facing the mountains.

"When did you do this?" she asks, turning to me.

"Had Carson drop them off while we were at work," I explain. "Thought it might be nice to have somewhere we could sit together to watch the sunset and enjoy the view."

She stares at the chairs for a long moment, then back at me, her eyes suspiciously bright. "You did this for us? For...for the future?"

The question holds weight, with implications that should frighten me but somehow don't. "Yeah," I answer honestly. "I did. I hope we can have quiet nights together, taking in the views. For as long as you want."

She reaches across the space between us, her hand finding my cheek. "I'd like that," she whispers. "I'd like that very much."

As I lean in to kiss her, I push away thoughts of Noah and cattle rustling and all the complications that threaten what we're building. For now, I just want to be a man with a woman he cares about, sitting on the porch watching the stars come out. The rest can wait until tomorrow.

ELEVEN
ATLEE

THE PAST TWO weeks have gone off without a hitch while Devlin and I have settled into a routine. We get up and get dressed as a couple. Sometimes we have breakfast, and then we leave at the same time—me in the used SUV that Devlin bought for me last week, and him in his truck. He heads to the Grizzly River Ranch for the day, and I head into town.

Then, at the end of the day, we show up at about the same time. We cook dinner together, eat, and then spend some time out on the back porch before coming in to shower and then watching some TV.

I never knew that life could be this settled, this happy. I've never had this kind of contentment in my life, and I love it more than I'm willing to admit to anyone. I'm leaning over the counter at Murphy's when I see Lennon walk in. "Hey," I wave at her, moving out and running up to hug her.

She hugs me tightly. "Hey, yourself. I came to see if you wanna go to the Rusty Spur tonight? Aubree and I are meeting over there for a drink, and I haven't been able to hang out with you much lately."

She's right. We haven't been able to hang out. Part of that is me. I haven't wanted to change my routine, because I'm in the honeymoon phase of my relationship with Devlin. The other part is that I'm still processing everything that happened with the robbery.

"I don't know," I hesitate, tucking a strand of hair behind my ear. "I should probably let Devlin know."

Lennon rolls her eyes. "You can text him while we're on the way. Come on, Atlee. I miss my sister. And it's not like I'm asking you to ditch him for a week. It's just a few hours."

I feel a pang of guilt. I have been neglecting Lennon. The past few weeks have been like living in a bubble with Devlin, warm and safe and separate from the rest of the world. But Lennon has been there for me through everything. She deserves better.

"What time?" I ask, already knowing I'm going to say yes.

Her face lights up. "We're meeting at eight. And before you start worrying about what to wear..." She holds up a hand to stop my protest. "I have clothes you can borrow. I'll swing by your work when your shift ends, and we can get ready at my place."

I glance down at my scrubs. "Yeah, these probably aren't Rusty Spur appropriate."

"Definitely not." Lennon laughs. "So you'll come?"

"Yeah, I'll come."

She pulls me into another hug. "Good. Because Aubree will kill me if I show up alone again. She says I'm a terrible wingwoman."

"Aubree needs a wingwoman?" I ask, surprised. Aubree and

Jesse are so totally together. Did something happen that I wasn't told about?

"Not for herself," Lennon says with a dismissive wave. "For me. She thinks I need to 'get back out there,' whatever that means."

"Ah," I say, understanding now. Lennon hasn't dated anyone seriously since her breakup with Mark two years ago. "And how do you feel about that?"

She shrugs, trying to look nonchalant, but I can see the vulnerability in her eyes. "I don't know. Maybe it's time. But that's not what tonight is about. Tonight is about me getting to spend time with my little sister, who's been all wrapped up in her hot cowboy."

I feel my cheeks heat. "He is hot, isn't he?"

"Gross." Lennon laughs, pushing my shoulder gently. "I don't need to hear about how hot you think your boyfriend is. I'll see you at five, okay?"

"Okay," I agree, watching as she heads toward the exit. "Hey, Len?" I call after her.

She turns, eyebrows raised in question.

"Thanks for coming to get me."

Her expression softens. "Always, sis. Always."

After she leaves, I pull out my phone to text Devlin, letting him know about my change in plans.

Me
Lennon wants me to go to the Rusty Spur tonight with her and Aubree. Girls' night. That okay?

His response comes a minute later.

Devlin
Have fun. Text me when you're done,
I'll come get you if you want to drink.

I smile at my phone. He's always looking out for me, making sure I'm safe. It's still new enough to feel like a small miracle every time.

Me
Thanks. I'll let you know.

The rest of my shift passes in a blur of prescriptions and customers. By the time five o'clock rolls around, I'm practically bouncing with anticipation. I haven't been out anywhere besides work and Devlin's cabin since the robbery. The thought is both exciting and a little terrifying.

Lennon is waiting for me in the parking lot, leaning against her car, scrolling through her phone. She looks up when I approach, a smile spreading across her face.

"Ready for a makeover?" she asks, waggling her eyebrows.

"As ready as I'll ever be." I laugh, climbing into the passenger seat.

At Lennon's apartment, she immediately drags me to her closet, pulling out options for me to try on. We settle on a pair of high-waisted jeans that hug my curves and a deep blue top that brings out the color in my eyes. The bruising on my face has almost completely faded, needing only a light layer of concealer to cover.

"You look amazing," Lennon says, stepping back to admire her handiwork after helping me with my makeup. "Devlin won't know what hit him."

"Devlin's not going to be there," I remind her. "Girls' night, remember?"

She gives me a knowing look. "Sure. And I'm the Queen of England."

"What's that supposed to mean?"

"It means Aubree is dating Jesse, who is Devlin's brother, and the Rusty Spur is where all the ranch hands go after work. So unless Devlin is planning to sit at home alone while his brother and all his friends are out having fun..."

I hadn't thought of that. "Oh."

"Don't worry," Lennon assures me, applying a final coat of mascara to her own lashes. "I'm not going to get mad if your hot cowboy shows up. Just don't ditch me the minute he walks in, okay?"

"Deal," I promise, feeling a flutter of anticipation at the thought of seeing Devlin in a social setting. We've been so wrapped up in our own little world, I haven't really seen him interact with many people besides Jesse and Aubree.

The Rusty Spur is already crowded when we arrive. Country music blasts from the speakers, and the dance floor is packed with couples two-stepping. Aubree waves to us from a table near the bar, and we weave our way through the crowd to join her.

"You made it!" she exclaims, standing to give me a hug. "And you look fantastic!"

"All Lennon's doing," I say, gesturing to my outfit. "She's the fashion expert."

"Well, she did good," Aubree says approvingly. "First round's on me. What are you having?"

"Just a beer for me," Lennon says.

"I'll have the same," I add.

Aubree flags down a waitress and orders three beers. "So," she says, turning back to us once the waitress leaves. "How's life with the mysterious Devlin? Still going well?"

"Really well," I admit, unable to keep the smile from my face. "It's...easy being with him. I never expected that."

"The Nelson men can be intense," Aubree agrees. "But they're good guys under all that brooding. It just takes the right woman to bring it out of them."

"And you're definitely bringing it out of Devlin," Lennon adds. "I've never seen him so...human."

I laugh at her description. "He's always been human, Len."

"Could've fooled me," she mutters, but there's no real heat behind it. "Before you, I don't think I ever heard him string more than three words together."

Our beers arrive, and we clink bottles in a toast. "To girls' night," Aubree says. "Long overdue."

"To girls' night," Lennon and I echo.

One beer turns into two, and then someone orders a round of tequila shots. The music gets louder, the crowd gets rowdier, and I find myself relaxing in a way I haven't in weeks. It feels good to laugh with my sister, to exchange stories with Aubree, and to just be a normal twenty-something woman out with friends.

"Oh my god," Aubree suddenly says, her eyes fixed on the entrance. "They're here."

Lennon and I turn to look. Jesse and Devlin are making their way through the crowd, and with them is Carson, Jesse, and Devlin's younger brother. Devlin's eyes scan the room, and when they land on me, his whole face changes. The hard lines soften, his lips curve into a smile, and something warm and possessive enters his gaze.

My heart does a little flip in my chest. Two weeks of sleeping beside him every night, and he still has the power to make me feel like a teenager with her first crush.

"Told you," Lennon says, nudging me with her elbow. "Predictable."

But I notice she's sitting up a little straighter, running a hand through her hair as the men approach, and her eyes aren't on Devlin or Jesse. They're fixed on Carson.

Interesting.

"Ladies," Jesse greets us, bending to kiss Aubree briefly. "Hope you don't mind us crashing your party."

"Not at all," Aubree says, making room for him beside her. "The more, the merrier."

Devlin slides into the seat next to me, his thigh pressing against mine under the table. "Having fun?" he asks, his voice low enough that only I can hear.

"Yeah," I say honestly. "It's good to get out."

His hand finds mine under the table, giving it a gentle squeeze. "You look beautiful," he murmurs, and I feel heat rise to my cheeks.

Carson, meanwhile, has taken the empty seat beside Lennon. "Lennon," he says, a slight drawl in his voice. "Didn't expect to see you here tonight."

"Why not?" she challenges, but there's a playful glint in her eye. "I do leave the office occasionally."

"Could've fooled me," he says with a grin. "Last time I stopped by, Shawn said you were chained to your desk reviewing depositions."

"Well, I'm here now," she says, taking a deliberate sip of her beer. "And I'm off the clock."

The tension between them is palpable, charging the air like lightning before a storm. I catch Aubree's eye across the table, and she gives me a smirk. What the fuck is going on with my sister and Carson?

Another round of drinks appears, and the conversation flows easily. Jesse talks about the progress on the barn renovation, Aubree shares stories from her office, and Carson keeps making comments that make Lennon either laugh or roll her eyes, sometimes both. It's nice being surrounded by people who care about each other, who care about me.

When a slow song starts playing, Devlin stands, holding out his hand to me. "Dance with me?"

I take his hand, letting him lead me to the dance floor. His arms wrap around my waist, pulling me close against his chest as we begin to sway to the music. I rest my head against his shoulder, breathing in the familiar scent of him, soap and leather and spice that make up Devlin.

"Thank you for coming to get me that day," I say, the words slipping out before I can stop them. Maybe it's the alcohol, or maybe it's just being here, surrounded by life and laughter after coming so close to losing everything.

He pulls back slightly, looking down at me with those intense eyes of his. "You don't have to thank me for that, Atlee. Ever."

"I know," I say. "But I wanted to anyway. I don't know what would have happened if—"

"Don't," he cuts me off gently. "Don't go there. You're here, you're safe, and that's all that matters."

I nod and swallow the lump in my throat. "I'm just...I'm happy, Devlin. Really happy."

Something flashes across his face, too quick for me to interpret. But then he's bending down, his lips finding mine in a kiss that makes my toes curl. It's not our most heated kiss, but there's something in it, a tenderness and a promise that leaves me breathless.

"I need to use the restroom," I murmur against his lips when we finally break apart. "I'll be right back."

He nods, reluctantly letting me go. I weave through the crowd toward the back of the bar, where the restrooms are located. The music is slightly muffled here, the lighting dimmer. I push open the door to the women's restroom, grateful to find it empty.

After taking care of business, I wash my hands and check my reflection in the mirror. My cheeks are flushed, and my eyes are bright—from the alcohol, from the dancing, from Devlin. I look happy. I am happy.

I'm still smiling as I exit the restroom, but the smile falters when I find Deputy Noah Sanchez leaning against the wall directly across from the door.

"Miss Walsh," he says, straightening up. "Just the person I was hoping to run into."

My stomach clenches. I've seen Noah watching Devlin, seen the tension between them, but we've never actually spoken. "Deputy," I acknowledge, trying to step around him.

He moves to block my path. "I'd like a word, if you don't mind."

I do mind, but I can tell from the set of his jaw that he's not going to let this go. "What can I help you with, Deputy?"

"It's more about what I can help you with," he says, his voice low and serious. "Do you know what you're dealing with? With Devlin Nelson?"

The question catches me off guard. "Excuse me?"

"I'm concerned for your safety," Noah continues. "The Nelson brothers are dangerous men, Miss Walsh. They're involved in things you don't want to be associated with."

"I don't know what you're talking about," I say, my heart beginning to race.

Noah's eyes narrow. He takes a step closer, lowering his voice further. "Listen, I'm not trying to scare you, but you seem like a good person who's already been through enough trouble. You should know who you're getting involved with."

"And who is that, exactly?" I challenge, anger beginning to replace my initial fear.

"Criminals," Noah says bluntly. "I can't say more than that right now, but trust me, you don't want to be caught in the middle when everything comes to light."

Before I can respond, a familiar voice cuts through the tension. "Problem here, Deputy?"

Devlin appears beside me, his body radiating barely controlled anger. His hand comes to rest at the small of my back, a gesture that's both protective and possessive.

Noah straightens, his gaze hardening as it shifts to Devlin. "Just having a friendly conversation with Miss Walsh here."

"Didn't look friendly to me," Devlin says, his voice dangerously calm. "Looked like you were cornering my girlfriend in a dark hallway. Not very professional."

His girlfriend? That's the first time he's ever called me that.

"Just doing my job," Noah replies. "Making sure the citizens of Grizzly River are safe."

"Is that right?" Devlin steps forward, putting himself between Noah and me. "Let me make something clear, Sanchez. You can try whatever you want with me, but you leave Atlee out of it. You want to intimidate someone? Try me. But you don't approach her, you don't talk to her, you don't even look at her sideways. Got it?"

Noah doesn't back down. "Are you threatening an officer of the law, Nelson?"

"I'm making a promise," Devlin says, his voice dropping even lower. "You want a war? You've got it. But keep it between us."

The two men stand toe-to-toe, the tension between them crackling like a live wire. For a moment, I think it might actually come to blows. Then Noah takes a deliberate step back.

"This isn't over," he says, his eyes flicking between Devlin and me. "Not by a long shot." With that, he turns and walks away, disappearing into the crowd.

Devlin turns to me immediately, his hands coming up to cup my face. "Are you okay? What did he say to you?"

I take a deep breath, trying to process what just happened. "He...he was warning me about you. Said you were dangerous, that you're involved in something illegal."

A muscle tics in Devlin's jaw. "It's complicated," he says after a moment. "But I swear to you, Atlee, I would never let anything happen to you. You know that, right?"

I nod, because I do know it. Whatever Devlin is involved in, whatever secrets he's keeping, I trust that his feelings for me are real. That his protection is real.

"Do you want to go home?" he asks softly.

I glance toward our table, where Lennon is laughing at something Carson said, where Jesse and Aubree are wrapped up in each other. Despite what just happened, I don't want to leave. I don't want Noah Sanchez to have that power.

"No," I decide. "I want to stay. I want to finish my night out with my sister and our friends."

A smile tugs at the corner of Devlin's mouth. "That's my girl," he says, pressing a kiss to my forehead. "But we're going to talk about this later."

"Yes," I agree, taking his hand. "We are."

As we walk back to the table, I can't help but wonder what I've gotten myself into. Whatever is going on between Devlin and Noah goes deeper than simple dislike. There's history there, secrets that I'm only just beginning to glimpse the edges of.

But as Devlin's hand tightens around mine, as he pulls out my chair for me and slides in beside me, his thigh once again pressed against mine, I know one thing for certain. I'm not walking away. Whatever storm is coming, we'll weather it together.

For better or worse, Devlin has become my home, and I'll fight like hell to protect what we're building, just as fiercely as he's fighting to protect me.

TWELVE
DEVLIN

THE NEXT MORNING, I'm waiting to meet Jesse, Truett, and Carson in the Grizzly River Ranch barn. After we got home last night, and I tucked Atlee into bed, I texted the guys and told them we needed to have a serious conversation about Noah.

I'm sitting with my back against one of the horse stalls, sipping on my coffee, when the guys start slowly making their way in. First comes Truett, rubbing his face with his free hand. "Is there a reason you wanted to do this so fuckin' early?"

"Didn't want any of the ranch hands to see us, and Atlee had to be at work early anyway."

He snorts. "Of course, it all comes back to Atlee."

I finish taking a drink of coffee and give him a smirk. "Same way all of yours comes back to Nora."

"Smart ass." He doesn't say anything else while we wait for Jesse and Carson.

Once we're all here, I give them a rundown of what I heard Noah say to Atlee last night. "He's looking for a reason, y'all. He knows he saw something that night, and he's not going to stop until he gets us."

"But we're not rustling anymore," Jesse argues. "We got rid of the cattle that had the different brands. We've covered our tracks, and now we're committed to being legit. No matter how difficult that's going to be."

Truett grunts his agreement. "We have a little bit of savings to fall back on, but we have to make sure we're prepared for next year. None of us wants to have to go back to where we started next year."

"We've got the money from the land sale," I remind them. "And we sold off fifteen acres too. For the first time since we took over our parents' ranches, we actually have money. We just have to be smart with it."

Carson clears his throat. "So if he asks where we got our money, we do have a cover story with that. You can't deny we sold land, and that land was worth the money we got for it."

I inhale deeply before blowing out a breath. "But he's got his suspicions, and no matter how careful we've been, there are cameras everywhere these days. We really need to figure out what he's got."

"I could hack in," Carson offers, moving his neck back and forth on his shoulders. "I haven't done it in a while, but y'all know how I used to love to do it as a teenager."

We do. He got in trouble and barely escaped jail time. "I don't know." I rub at the whiskers on my jaw. "What do y'all think?"

Truett takes a drink of his coffee. "Can't hurt. I mean, just make sure it can't be traced back to you or us."

There's a part of me that wants to tell them all that we don't need this. We're legit now, and all we have to do is move past what we were doing previously. The other part of me that knows we have to be prepared and never goes into an op without knowing what I am facing, knows this is the right thing to do. "All right," I agree.

Carson finishes his coffee. "Give me the day off. I'll be back to let y'all know what we're facing."

"Go," Jesse tells him. "Get it done as quickly as possible and then get your ass back here."

Carson nods, already turning to leave. He's always been the tech guy in our operation, the one who could make anything digital work for us. If anyone can figure out what Noah has on us, it's him.

As he walks out, Truett grabs my arm. "Follow him," he says quietly, making sure Jesse can't hear. "Not because I don't trust him, but because if something goes wrong, he needs backup."

I study Truett's face. The concern there is real. Carson might be the smartest of us all, but he's also the most reckless. "Yeah," I agree. "Good call."

Jesse is organizing feed bags on the far side of the barn, and I head over to him. "I'm gonna head into town," I tell him. "Got some errands to run."

He looks up, wiping sweat from his forehead. "Now? We've got work to do here."

"It's important," I say, keeping my voice low. "Trust me on this."

Something in my tone must convince him, because he nods after a moment. "All right. But be back by afternoon. We've got that fence in the north pasture to mend."

"Will do." I clap him on the shoulder and head out, careful to take my time so it doesn't look like I'm following Carson.

By the time I get to my truck, Carson has already disappeared down the road in his beat-up Chevy. I give him a five-minute head start before following. The road into Grizzly River is long and winding, making it easy to keep a decent distance while still keeping him in sight.

When we hit the town limits, Carson doesn't head toward the library like I expected. Instead, he drives to the edge of town, pulling up outside a rundown warehouse that used to be a distribution center for farm equipment. It's been abandoned for years, but rumor has it some tech company bought it recently, planning to turn it into a server farm or something.

I park a block away, watching as Carson gets out of his truck and heads inside, looking over his shoulder twice before slipping through a side door. Interesting choice of location. It must have better internet than his place at the ranch.

Now I need a cover story for being in town. Atlee is working at the pharmacy today, and it's almost lunchtime. Perfect.

I drive over to Murphy's General Store, parking right out front where anyone passing by can see my truck. Inside, the store is busy with the usual morning crowd. I make my way to the pharmacy section at the back, nodding at a few people who recognize me.

Atlee is behind the counter, her dark hair pulled back in a neat ponytail, wearing those blue scrubs that somehow make her look both professional and sexy as hell. She's helping an elderly woman with her medication, her face focused and serious. She hasn't seen me yet.

I lean against the counter, waiting until she finishes with her customer. When she turns and spots me, her whole face lights up, and damn if that doesn't do something to my insides.

"Devlin," she says, surprise and pleasure in her voice. "What are you doing here?"

"Thought I'd take my girl to lunch," I say, keeping my voice casual despite the warmth spreading through my chest at the way she's looking at me. "If she can get away for an hour."

She glances at the clock on the wall. "I was just about to take my break." Her eyes meet mine, a smile playing at the corners of her mouth. "Lucky timing."

"Very lucky," I agree, watching as she tells her coworker she's heading out for lunch.

She comes around the counter, and I resist the urge to pull her into my arms right there in the middle of the store. We're still figuring out what we are to each other, but in this small town, people talk, and with Noah sniffing around, I don't want to give anyone more ammunition.

"Where are we going?" she asks as we head outside.

"The diner," I say, placing my hand on the small of her back as we walk to my truck. It's a possessive gesture, one that marks her as mine to anyone watching. "Thought we could get some of those burgers you like."

"You remembered," she says, looking pleased.

We talked about it on our ride together to get the medication for Truett. "I remember everything about you." The words come out before I can stop them, more honest than I intended.

She blushes, climbing into the passenger seat of my truck. "Smooth talker."

I grin, closing her door and walking around to my side. As I start the engine, I scan the street, looking for any sign of Noah or his patrol car. Nothing yet.

The diner is the busiest lunch spot in town, which is exactly why I chose it. The more people who see us together, acting like a normal couple, the better. It helps solidify our cover and makes it clear I'm not up to anything suspicious. I'm just a man taking his woman out for a meal.

We're seated in a booth by the window, prime real estate for being seen. Atlee doesn't seem to notice my strategic choice of seating, already looking over the menu.

"So," she says, setting down her menu. "Not that I'm complaining, but what brought this on? You don't usually show up at work."

"Can't a man surprise his woman?" I counter, reaching across the table to take her hand.

She tilts her head, those blue eyes of hers too perceptive for comfort. "He can. But I get the feeling there's more to it."

Damn, she's good. "Maybe I just missed you," I say, which isn't a lie. Even though we live together and sleep in the same bed, I find myself thinking about her when we're apart. It's pathetic, really, how much I've come to need her presence in my life.

Her expression softens. "I missed you too." She squeezes my hand. "But seriously, is everything okay? After last night with Noah—"

"Everything's fine," I interrupt, not wanting her to worry. "Noah's just a pain in the ass with a chip on his shoulder."

She looks like she wants to say more, but the waitress arrives to take our order. As predicted, Atlee gets a burger. I order the same, plus a side of chili fries for us to share.

As we wait for our food, I keep one eye on the door, watching for Noah. It's his usual lunch hour, and the diner is one of his regular spots. Sure enough, just as our food arrives, the bell above the door jingles and in he walks, uniform crisp, expression sour as usual.

His eyes scan the room, landing on us almost immediately. I feel Atlee tense across from me, her gaze following mine.

"Don't look," I murmur, reaching across the table to tuck a strand of hair behind her ear. The gesture is intimate, deliberate, meant to be seen. "Just focus on me."

She nods slightly, but I can see the question in her eyes. I'll have to explain this later, but for now, I need her to follow my lead.

"So," I say, loud enough to be heard at nearby tables. "I was thinking we could go away this weekend. Just the two of us. Maybe drive up to that bed-and-breakfast I heard you talking to Lennon about."

Her eyes widen slightly at my uncharacteristic volume, but she catches on quickly. "The one in Black Hills? With the hot tubs in each room? You heard me talking to her about that?"

"Yeah, I did. That's the one," I say, letting my voice drop to a suggestive tone as I run my thumb across her knuckles. "Thought we could use some alone time."

She blushes, but plays along, leaning forward slightly. "I'd like that."

Out of the corner of my eye, I see Noah being seated a few tables away, directly in my line of sight. Perfect. I keep my focus on Atlee, but I know he's watching us, his disapproval practically radiating across the room.

I feed Atlee a chili fry, making her laugh when I deliberately miss her mouth and smear sauce on her chin. As I reach over with a napkin to wipe it off, I let my gaze lock with Noah's across the room. The challenge in my stare is clear—she's with me, and there's nothing you can do about it. He might want to warn her away again, but it's not going to matter. Atlee trusts me more than she's ever trusted anyone else, and I'm not letting that go.

His jaw tightens, but he looks away first. Small victories.

By the time we finish eating, half the town has seen us together, laughing and touching and looking every bit the happy couple.

As we're waiting for the check, my phone buzzes with a text from Carson.

Carson
Heading back to the ranch. Got what we need.

I feel a mixture of relief and tension. On one hand, it's good that he's managed to get whatever information he was after. On the other, now we'll know exactly what we're facing with Noah.

"We should get you back," I tell Atlee, leaving cash on the table to cover our meal. "Don't want you to be late."

She nods, sliding out of the booth. As we pass Noah's table, I place my hand on the small of Atlee's back again, a clear signal of possession. She doesn't seem to mind, leaning into me slightly.

Noah doesn't look up, but his knuckles are white around his fork.

Outside, I help Atlee into the truck, using the opportunity to steal a quick kiss. "Thanks for lunch," she says, smiling up at me. "It was a nice surprise."

"Anytime," I say, and mean it. Despite the ulterior motives for today's visit, being with her is never a hardship.

I drive her back to the pharmacy, keeping an eye on the rearview mirror for any sign of a patrol car following us. Nothing yet, but I wouldn't put it past Noah to try to tail me after I drop her off.

"See you at home?" she asks as I pull up in front of Murphy's.

I love that she's started to call the cabin home. At some point, I'm going to need to talk to her about letting her apartment go. I'm thinking of her being there as being my home too, and I don't want to ever let it go.

"Count on it," I say, giving her one more kiss before she slides out of the truck.

I wait until she's safely inside before pulling away. Instead of heading straight back to the ranch, I take a roundabout route, watching for any cars that might be following me. When I'm satisfied I'm alone, I head toward the edge of town where I last saw Carson.

Sure enough, his truck is just pulling out from the side street near the warehouse. I hang back, letting him get a good head start before following at a distance. The last thing we need is for Noah to catch us together, especially coming from that particular location.

Carson seems oblivious to my presence behind him, driving at his usual reckless speed back toward the ranch. I keep a safe distance, scanning both the road ahead and my mirrors regularly. About halfway back, I spot a flash of white and blue in my rearview, a patrol car, too far back to make out the driver, but heading in our direction.

Shit. I slow down, letting Carson pull further ahead while I watch the patrol car gain ground behind me. If it's Noah, I can't let him see me following Carson. I need to create some distance, so he can't even see Carson.

There's a turnoff coming up that leads to a scenic overlook. At the last second, I signal and pull off, like I've decided on a whim to take in the view. The patrol car zooms past without slowing. Through the window, I catch a glimpse of the driver. It's not Noah, but his partner, Deputy Michaels. Still, better safe than sorry.

I wait a full five minutes before pulling back onto the main road. By now, Carson should be close to the ranch. The rest of the drive is uneventful, my thoughts split between what Carson might have discovered and the memory of Atlee's smile across the lunch table.

When I finally pull up to the ranch house, Jesse is waiting on the porch, arms crossed over his chest.

"You're late," he says as I climb out of my truck. "Fence isn't going to fix itself."

"Had to take a detour," I explain, nodding toward the barn. "Carson back yet?"

Jesse's expression turns serious. "Yeah, he's waiting for us. Says he found something we all need to see."

My gut clenches. Whatever Carson discovered, I have a feeling our lives are about to get a lot more complicated. And with Atlee now firmly in the picture, the stakes have never been higher.

"Let's go hear what he's got," I say, following Jesse toward the barn where our future, and possibly our freedom, hangs in the balance.

THIRTEEN
ATLEE

LUNCH WITH DEVLIN WAS FUN. I didn't expect him to show up and treat me to it, but when I saw Noah walk into the diner, I knew there was a reason for us to be there, especially after what he said to me the night at the bar.

Payton comes over and gives me a smile. "You and Devlin seem to be getting along well."

I'm not sure if I'm comfortable discussing my relationship with Devlin with other people, but I feel the need to sing his praises. "We are. I haven't been back to my apartment since he came and saved me. Maybe I should?" I pull my thumbnail in between my teeth as I say the words.

"Why do you think you should? If the two of you are happy, then what does it matter?" Payton lifts her shoulders up. "If I had someone as hot as him in my home, in my bed, and looking at me the way he looks at you, I wouldn't be looking for a reason to get rid of him, Atlee. If you're happy, fuck anyone who questions it."

As she says the words, I spot Noah's patrol car slow rolling by the pharmacy. Anxiousness creeps up in my stomach, but I try to push it away. Shaking my head, I paste a smile on my face and glance over at Payton. "You're right. We're good. Fuck anyone who doesn't understand it."

Payton squeezes my shoulder before heading back to her station. I try to focus on filling prescriptions for the rest of my shift, but my mind keeps wandering back to Noah's warning and the tension between him and Devlin. It has to be more than Devlin stealing his girlfriend in high school. I know it's more than that. I'm not stupid, but at the same time, I don't want to look too closely.

But every time doubt creeps in, I push it away. I know Devlin. At least, I know the man he is with me—protective, gentle when it matters, rough when I want it. He makes me feel safe in a way I've never experienced before. Whatever Noah thinks he knows, he doesn't know that part of Devlin.

The rest of the afternoon drags by, with customers coming and going in a steady stream. I'm grateful for the distraction, for the routine of measuring medications, answering questions, and offering advice. It's familiar territory, something I can control when so much else feels uncertain.

By the time five o'clock rolls around, I'm more than ready to leave. The sky outside has turned a deep purple, the sun already setting behind the mountains. I grab my coat from the back room, wrapping it tightly around myself as I step outside.

The cold hits me immediately, a sharp contrast to the heated interior of the store. Winter is coming early this year. I can feel it in the bite of the wind and see it in the heavy clouds gathering on the horizon. The first real snow isn't far off.

I hurry to my SUV, the one Devlin bought me when I told him that I was walking back and forth to work. It's nothing fancy, just a used model with decent mileage, but it's the most expensive gift anyone's ever given me. I still feel a flutter of something warm and complicated whenever I slide behind the wheel. In my childhood, gifts were used to manipulate, and I pray with everything I have that's not why Devlin did this for me.

The engine starts with a satisfying rumble, and I crank the heat up to full blast, holding my hands in front of the vents while I wait for it to warm up. The thought of driving these winding mountain roads in snow sends a chill down my spine that has nothing to do with the temperature.

It's going to be a bitch getting to and from Devlin's place when winter really sets in.

The thought stops me short. I've been automatically thinking about staying with Devlin through the winter and not going back to my apartment at all. When did that happen? When did I start planning a future with this man without even discussing it with him?

We've never said "I love you" to each other. We've never even had a conversation about what we are to each other beyond our day-to-day life right now. Yet here I am, mentally rearranging my entire life as if it's a foregone conclusion that we're in this for the long haul.

The crazy thing is, it feels right. I've only had a couple of other boyfriends, but all of them made me feel like I did with my family growing up. Like I didn't belong. Like I was trying to force my round body into a square peg, and I could never be me. With Devlin, it's different. Despite how quickly it's all happened, despite the trauma that brought us together, being with him feels like the most natural thing in the world.

I put the car in drive and pull out of the parking lot, my mind still turning over these realizations as I head toward the ranch. The road stretches out before me, winding up into the hills where Devlin's cabin waits—my port in the storm of my emotions. He and I really need to have a conversation about where all of this is going. I can't be making plans when he may not even be thinking the same way I am.

About four miles from the turnoff to his place, I notice headlights in my rearview mirror. They've been behind me for a while, keeping a steady distance. Nothing unusual about that. There are only so many roads out this way, but something about it makes the hair on the back of my neck stand up.

I slow down a little, expecting the car to pass, but it slows too, maintaining the exact same distance. My pulse quickens. I'm being paranoid, I tell myself. The robbery has made me jumpy, seeing threats where there are none. I should probably be on some sort of anti-anxiety medication at this point. I'm seeing shit where there is none.

Just as I'm about to speed up again, blue and red lights flash in my mirror, accompanied by a short burst from a siren. My stomach drops as I signal and pull over to the side of the road, gravel crunching under my tires.

Deputy Noah Sanchez. Because of course it's him.

I take a deep breath, trying to calm my racing heart as I watch him approach in the side mirror. He takes his time, touching the back near the trunk, making a show of checking out my vehicle, shining his flashlight around the exterior before finally coming to my window.

I roll it down, letting in a blast of cold air. "Deputy," I greet him, aiming for polite but falling somewhere around wary.

"Miss Walsh," he says, his face impassive in the harsh beam of his flashlight. "License and registration, please."

I fumble in my purse for my wallet, then reach across to the glove compartment for the registration, hoping like fuck it's there. I never asked Devlin. "Is there a problem?" I ask, breathing easier when I find the registration, and then hand over the documents.

"You were doing forty in a thirty-five," he says, examining my license with unnecessary thoroughness. "A little fast for these roads, especially with night coming on."

Five miles over. He pulled me over for going five miles over the speed limit. We both know this isn't about my driving. What a fucking asshole.

"I'll be more careful," I say, keeping my tone neutral. No point in antagonizing him and making more trouble for myself. I've never actually been pulled over before, so this makes me more nervous than I care to admit.

He hands back my license but keeps the registration. "This vehicle is registered to Devlin Nelson."

It's not a question, but I answer anyway. "He bought it for me after my car broke down." That's the simplest way to explain the situation.

"That's mighty generous," Noah says, something unreadable flickering across his face. "Must be nice, having someone who can afford gifts like that."

I say nothing, waiting for him to get to the point.

"You know," he continues, leaning down so his face is level with mine. "I've been looking into the Nelson brothers and their friend Truett. Interesting trio. All of them struggling with their ranches for years, barely keeping afloat. Then suddenly, they've got money. New equipment, repairs on both the main house, fancy cars for their girlfriends."

This isn't a fucking fancy car, and he knows it.

"Deputy—"

"And at the same time," he talks over me. "We've had a rash of cattle rustling across three counties. Small numbers, different brands, but it adds up. Almost like someone's been careful not to take too much from any one place."

My mouth goes dry. Cattle rustling? "I don't know anything about that."

"No?" He straightens up, towering over me. "Well, maybe you should ask your boyfriend where all his sudden wealth came from. Because I'm telling you, Miss Walsh, those men are headed for trouble, and anyone standing too close when it all comes down is going to get burned."

I grip the steering wheel tighter, trying to keep my voice steady. I have no idea what he means by sudden wealth. All I can tell from looking around at the ranch is that it looks like they're coming out of a bad spot. But at the same time, Devlin is ex-military, which means he's probably getting paid by them every month, along with the money he makes at the ranch. But I don't know, because I never asked. "Are you going to give me a ticket, Deputy? Or is this just a courtesy warning about my speed?"

His lips thin into a tight line. "Warning this time," he says finally. "But you be careful out there, Miss Walsh. Roads like these, things can happen."

The implied threat hangs in the air between us. He hands back my registration and takes a step back from the car.

Just as he does, another vehicle pulls up behind his patrol car, its headlights cutting through the growing darkness. Noah turns, his hand automatically going to his holster before relaxing when he recognizes the driver emerging from the pickup truck.

My blood runs cold as I recognize him too. Richard Morrison, the oldest of the Morrison brothers, whose family owns one of the bigger ranches in the county. He's a big man with cold eyes, and he's looking right at me before turning his attention to Noah.

"Everything all right here, Deputy?" Morrison calls out, his voice carrying on the cold air. "Saw your lights and thought I'd check."

"Just a routine stop, Mr. Morrison," Noah answers, his tone suddenly deferential. "All wrapped up now."

Morrison nods, his gaze shifting back to me for a beat too long before returning to Noah. "Good to hear. Say, why don't you stop by the ranch later? Got some concerns about trespassers I'd like to discuss. Maybe something to do with the people who stole our cattle."

"Will do, sir," Noah responds.

The exchange is brief, seemingly innocent, but something about it sends a chill through me that has nothing to do with the cold. The way Morrison looked at me, like he was committing my face to memory. The way Noah's whole demeanor changed in his presence.

I roll up my window as Noah heads back to his patrol car, not waiting for him to dismiss me. In my mirror, I watch as

Morrison says something else to Noah, too low for me to hear, both of them glancing in my direction.

As soon as Noah's lights go off, I pull back onto the road, my hands shaking slightly on the wheel. I don't relax until both their vehicles are out of sight in my rearview mirror.

My mind is racing. Everything that just happened plays over and over again.

If what Noah is suggesting is true...if Devlin, Jesse, and Truett have been stealing cattle.

No. I can't believe that. I won't believe it. There has to be another explanation.

But I need to tell Devlin about this encounter. About Morrison showing up, about the way he looked at me. Whatever's going on, I need to know that I'm not walking blindly into something that could blow up in my face.

The rest of the drive to the cabin passes in a blur of anxiety and questions. By the time I pull up at Devlin's place, my nerves are stretched thin. I love this man, even if I haven't said the words out loud yet, and I trust him. But that doesn't mean I don't deserve the truth.

As I step out into the cold evening air, I make a promise to myself. Tonight, I'm going to get answers, one way or another. Because whatever storm is coming, I need to know exactly what we're facing, together.

FOURTEEN
DEVLIN

WE'VE all set up in the barn, waiting to see what Carson found out for us. One of the things I prided myself on when I was in the military was that I didn't get nervous—not when we were in trouble, and not when I had someone pointing a gun at my head, asking me to betray my squad.

But this? I'm nervous about this.

Whatever we find out from Carson is going to potentially change our immediate future. After all of us get situated, and Carson pulls out a laptop, we give him our attention.

"There's a lot of information here," he starts, folding his arms over his chest. "There's some of it I don't actually understand, but I think we may have made a mistake messing with the Morrison Ranch."

"I think you did too."

We all turn around to the entrance, me faster than the rest of them, because that voice belongs to Atlee. "What the hell?"

She runs her hands through her hair and then tells us about

the run-in she just had with Deputy Sanchez. "I'm sorry I showed up here out of the blue, but when I got home and saw your truck wasn't there, I knew you were still here," she says as she grabs hold of my hand, entwining our fingers together. "I knew I had to tell you."

"You did the right thing." I lean down and place a kiss on her forehead.

The tension in the room is thick, and all of us are feeling the stress. Her eyes look back and forth between my brothers and Truett. "I can leave if you want me to," she offers. "I just wanted to make sure you knew. I don't have to stay here for the rest of it."

Truett curses, throwing his hands up in the air. "She might as well. That way she knows what we're up against too."

Carson clears his throat. "Okay, so back to what I found out today."

The way Atlee's hand tightens in mine tells me she's nervous, and I don't blame her. I squeeze back, trying to reassure her even though my own gut is in knots. I guide her over to a hay bale where we can sit.

"Go ahead," Jesse says to Carson, his voice tight. "What did you find?"

Carson opens his laptop, tapping a few keys before turning the screen so we can all see. "Noah's been building a case against us for months. He's methodical, I'll give him that."

On the screen, a grainy video shows a truck driving down a dark country road. The time stamp reads 2:14 a.m. from the night of the Morrison job.

"Doorbell camera from the Thompson place," Carson explains. "Two miles from the Morrison Ranch. This was the night we hit their south pasture."

I feel Atlee stiffen beside me, but I keep my eyes on the screen.

"And this," Carson continues, clicking to another video. "Traffic camera at the intersection of Route 16 and County Road 8. Same night, forty minutes later."

This footage is clearer, showing our truck with the livestock trailer behind it. My blood runs cold.

"Can they see the license plate?" Truett asks, voicing what we're all thinking.

Carson shakes his head. "It's too dark, and the angle's wrong. But the make and model match our truck."

"That's not enough," Jesse says. "Half the ranchers in the county drive the same truck."

"True," Carson agrees. "But there's more." He clicks through to a document, a police report filed by Richard Morrison. "Noah's got a statement from Morrison claiming he fired at rustlers on his property. He says he thinks he hit one of them."

I exchange a look with Truett, remembering the bullet that hit him that night. We'd told everyone it was from a fence repair gone wrong.

"There's something else," Carson says, his voice dropping lower. "Noah's been keeping detailed notes on all of us. Especially you, Devlin."

He clicks to another document, and my stomach drops when I see my name followed by Atlee's.

"He's been watching your relationship develop," Carson explains, scrolling through the file. "Documenting when you're together, where you go. He's got notes here about putting pressure on...on Atlee."

Atlee's grip on my hand is now almost painful. "What does that mean?" she asks, her voice barely above a whisper.

Carson looks uncomfortable. "He believes if he can get one of you to break, it'll be you. He's planning to use you to get to Devlin."

"Son of a bitch," I mutter, rage building in my chest.

"There's more," Carson continues. "Noah's been meeting regularly with Richard Morrison, and not just on official police business. They go way back. Morrison's been pushing him to make arrests, specifically targeting us."

"Why?" Jesse demands. "I mean, yeah, we took some of their cattle, but we hit other ranches too. Why are they so focused on us?"

Carson hesitates. "That's where it gets complicated. I found emails between Noah and Morrison discussing something called 'Project Watershed.' I couldn't access all the details, but it involves buying up land around Grizzly River, including sections that border our properties."

"Water rights," Truett says suddenly. "The drought's been getting worse every year. If they control the watershed..."

"They control who gets water," Jesse finishes, realization dawning on his face. "And without water..."

"Our ranches are worthless," I conclude. "So they want us gone."

"And what better way than to send us to prison for cattle rustling?" Carson adds.

The barn falls silent as the full weight of what we're facing sinks in. This isn't just about the cattle we stole. It's about our land, our future, everything our families have built for generations.

"How much time do we have?" I ask Carson.

He shakes his head. "Hard to say. Noah's being careful, building his case slowly. But based on his notes, he's getting ready to move soon. Weeks, maybe days."

I look down at Atlee, who's been quiet through most of this. Her face is pale, but her jaw is set in that stubborn way I've come to recognize. She's processing, not panicking.

"Atlee," I say softly, turning to face her fully. "You need to understand what this means. What I...what we've done."

"I think I've figured it out," she says, her voice steadier than I expected. "You've been stealing cattle."

I nod, not trying to deny it. "We were desperate. After our parents died, we had to take care of each other. There wasn't the money that there should've been. Both sets of our parents had mismanaged money, and we wanted to keep our families together. We had to keep them together."

"So you started rustling," she states, not a question.

"Just enough to keep the ranches afloat," Jesse interjects. "We never got greedy."

"And we stopped," I add quickly. "Once we sold land and got some breathing room, we shut it down. We're going legitimate now." I stop for a second. "But now I wonder who actually bought that land. Hopefully, they weren't connected to Morrison, and how does Noah fit into this?"

Atlee looks around at each of us, her expression unreadable. "And Noah knows? He has proof?"

"Seems like it. Proof is circumstantial," Carson answers. "But he's building something solid. And with Morrison backing him..."

"It's my fault," Truett says suddenly, running a hand through his hair. "I'm the one who suggested hitting the Morrison place. I thought they had so many head that they'd never notice a few missing."

"We all agreed," I remind him. "We're all in this together."

Atlee pulls her hand from mine, and for a moment, I think this is it, that she's going to walk away. But instead, she stands up and faces all of us.

"So what's the plan?" she asks, crossing her arms. "How do we fix this?"

The "we" doesn't escape my notice, and something shifts in my chest.

"Atlee," I say, standing to join her. "You don't have to be involved in this. In fact, you should probably stay as far away as possible. If Noah is targeting you..."

"I'm already involved," she cuts me off. "He pulled me over specifically to warn me about you. He's using me, whether I want to be or not."

"She's right," Carson says. "And having her on our side might actually help. Noah won't expect that."

I shake my head. "No. It's too dangerous. If things go south..."

"Then I'll be implicated anyway," Atlee argues. "Noah has already connected us. Running away now won't help either of us."

"She's got a point," Jesse says, earning him a glare from me.

"So what are our options?" Truett asks, bringing us back to the problem at hand.

Carson closes his laptop. "We need to find out more about this Project Watershed. If Morrison and Noah are up to something shady themselves, maybe we can use that as leverage."

"What about Lennon?" Atlee suggests. "She works for the best attorney in the state. Maybe she could help, or at least advise us."

The thought had crossed my mind too, but involving Atlee's sister means pulling another person into our mess. "Would she be willing to help, knowing what we've done? She offered, but I'm not sure if she realized it would involve this." I gesture around us.

Atlee hesitates. "I don't know. She's by the book in a lot of ways, but she's also fiercely loyal. If I asked her—"

"Let's keep that as a last resort," Jesse decides. "For now, we need more information. Carson, can you dig deeper into Project Watershed? Find out exactly what Morrison's planning?"

Carson nods. "I'll try, but I'll need to be careful. If they catch me snooping in their systems..."

"Take whatever precautions you need," Jesse tells him. "Truett, when you go to town to see Nora, see what you can find out."

Truett gives a mock salute. "Will do."

"And us?" I ask, gesturing between myself and Atlee.

Jesse thinks for a moment. "You two need to act normal. Go about your routines and don't give Noah any reason to suspect we're onto him."

"That includes being seen together in public," Truett adds. "If you suddenly start avoiding each other, it'll look suspicious."

I look down at Atlee, searching her face. "You okay with that? With keeping up appearances while we figure this out?"

She meets my eyes. "It won't be an act for me."

Those simple words hit me harder than I expected, causing a

tightness in my throat. Even knowing what she knows now, she's still here, still choosing to stand with me.

"We should head back to the cabin," I tell her. "It's getting late, and we've all got a lot to process."

She nods, and I can see the exhaustion setting in. It's been a long day for all of us.

"We'll meet again tomorrow night," Jesse tells everyone. "Same time, same place. Keep your phones on, but be careful what you say. Assume Noah is watching everything."

As we all prepare to leave, I pull Atlee aside, needing a moment alone with her. "Are you sure about this?" I ask, keeping my voice low. "It's okay if you want to leave, to distance yourself from all of this. From me."

She reaches up, placing her hand against my cheek. "I'm sure."

"Even knowing what I've done? What I'm capable of?"

"I've always known you were capable of more than you let on," she says with a small smile. "The question is, do you want me to stay? Now that I know everything, am I a liability?"

The thought of sending her away, of facing this without her, creates a hollow feeling in my chest I can't stand. "I want you with me," I admit. "But I need you safe more than I need you with me."

"Then let me decide what's safe for me," she counters. "I'm not walking away, Devlin. Not unless you tell me you don't want me here."

I pull her against me, burying my face in her hair. "I want you here," I whisper. "God help me, but I do."

I feel her relax against me, her arms tightening around my waist. "Then that's where I'll be."

As we walk out of the barn toward my truck, the weight of everything we're facing hangs heavy on my shoulders. But having Atlee beside me, knowing she's chosen to stay even after learning the truth, makes that weight bearable.

Whatever comes next, we'll face it together. And God help anyone who tries to come between us...Noah and Morrison included.

FIFTEEN
ATLEE

DEVLIN FOLLOWS ME HOME, his truck never leaving my rearview mirror. If there's anything about this man, it's that he's committed to making sure I'm safe. I love this about him. I love a lot about him, and I'm going to tell him that tonight.

As we pull around the back of Devlin's house, I gather my stuff, but before I can get out, he's already come over to the door and is opening it for me.

"Thank you." I smile up at him as he holds the door for me.

I get out, and he pins me up against the driver's side door. "You're welcome," he says, right before he takes my mouth in a steamy kiss. I let myself melt into him for a few moments before he pulls away. "I'm sorry about everything that happened tonight."

Reaching around his waist, I hug him tight. "I'm not, Devlin."

He looks like he wants to say more, a pained expression

crossing his face. "I just hope that you aren't doing this because you think I expect you to."

I shake my head, pulling back to look at him properly. The moonlight catches the sharp angles of his face, making him look both dangerous and vulnerable at the same time.

"I'm not doing anything because I think you expect it," I tell him firmly. "I'm here because I want to be."

He studies my face, like he's trying to read the truth in my expression. Whatever he sees there seems to satisfy him, at least temporarily.

"Let's go sit," he says, nodding toward the back porch and the rocking chairs that have become our nightly ritual.

I follow him, but instead of heading straight for the chairs, I find myself drawn to the railing. From here, the view of the mountains is breathtaking, even in the dark. The moon casts everything in silver.

"It's beautiful out here," I say softly, feeling him come up behind me. His arms wrap around my waist, and I lean back against his chest, soaking in his warmth against the chill of the night air.

"Yeah," he agrees, his voice rumbling against my back. "Never gets old."

We stand like that for a while, just breathing together, watching the night. There's so much I want to say, but the words feel heavy in my throat, weighted with importance.

"When I was a little girl," I start, surprising myself with where my mind has gone. "I used to imagine what my life would be like when I grew up. I'd dream about having a house with a white picket fence, a dog in the yard, someone who loved me waiting for me to come home."

His arms tighten around me slightly, but he doesn't interrupt.

"My parents weren't exactly the loving type," I continue, the familiar ache dulled by time and distance. "Dad was drunk more often than not, and Mom was too busy trying to keep him from flying off the handle to pay much attention to me or Lennon. We raised each other, really. I've told you a little bit about that. Enough for you to assume."

I turn in his arms, needing to see his face for what comes next. His eyes are dark and attentive, fixed on mine.

"I've been looking for something my entire life, Devlin," I tell him, my voice steady despite the vulnerability of the admission. "Something my parents never gave me. Love, security, a place where I belong. I kept thinking I'd find it—in school, at work, in other relationships—but it was never quite right. Never quite enough."

"Atlee..." He says my name like a prayer, his hands coming up to frame my face.

"I want to show you something," I whisper, taking his hand and leading him to the rocking chairs. When he sits, I don't take the chair beside him. Instead, I straddle his lap, facing him, my knees on either side of his thighs.

His hands automatically come to rest on my hips, steadying me, before they go around to palm my ass. The surprise in his eyes is quickly replaced by heat, but I need him to hear me before we get lost in each other.

I take his face between my palms, making sure he's looking right at me. "I've found it now," I tell him, my thumbs stroking the stubble on his cheeks. "With you. This feeling, this peace—

it's what I've been searching for all along. And I'm not letting it go, not for Noah, not for anyone."

His eyes widen slightly, like he can't quite believe what he's hearing. "Atlee, you don't know what you're saying. The trouble we could be in..."

"I know exactly what I'm saying," I cut him off. "I love you, Devlin. I love your strength and your gentleness. I love the way you make me feel safe without making me feel weak. I love that you built this place with your own hands, that you knew what you wanted and made it happen. I love all of it, the good and the bad."

He looks stunned, like I've knocked the wind out of him. His hands tighten on my hips, and for a moment, I worry I've said too much too soon. But then his expression shifts, a rawness I've never seen before breaking through.

"I'll do whatever it takes to protect what we have," I continue, the words spilling out now that I've started. "Whatever you need me to do, I'll do it. I'm all in, Devlin. All the way."

"Why?" he asks, his voice hoarse. "Why would you risk everything for me? I've done things, Atlee. Things I'm not proud of."

"Because that's what you do when you love someone," I tell him simply. "You stand by them. You fight for them."

His hand slides up my back, coming to rest at the nape of my neck. "You're incredible, you know that?" he murmurs. "Walking right into this mess with your eyes open, choosing to stay when most people would run."

"I'm not most people," I remind him with a small smile.

"No," he agrees, pulling me closer. "You're certainly not."

When his lips meet mine, it's different from the kiss we

shared by the car. That was heat and passion. This is deeper, something that feels like a promise. I melt against him, my body molding to his, my fingers threading through his hair.

He tastes both like danger and safety, and I can't get enough. I press closer, feeling the solid strength of him beneath me, the steady beat of his heart against my chest.

His hands slide under my shirt, warm against my skin, and I shiver at his touch. "Cold?" he asks against my lips.

"No," I breathe, rocking my hips against his. "Definitely not cold."

He groans, the sound vibrating through both of us. "We should go inside," he suggests, though his hands are still moving, exploring the curve of my waist, the dip of my spine. The rough tips of his fingers play over the edges of my shirt.

"Or we could stay right here," I counter, nipping at his bottom lip. "Under the stars."

His eyes darken at the suggestion, and I can feel his body's immediate response beneath me. "Out in the open? Feeling adventurous, aren't you?"

"There's no one around for miles," I remind him, grinding down deliberately. "And I want you, Devlin. Right here, right now."

That seems to break his restraint. With a growl, he captures my mouth in a searing kiss, his hands now moving with purpose, tugging at my clothing. I return the favor, fumbling with the buttons of his shirt, desperate to feel his skin against mine.

We undress each other with frantic need, pausing only to adjust our position so I'm still straddling him, but now we're both gloriously naked, the cool night air raising goose bumps on my exposed skin. But I hardly notice the cold, not with the heat building between us, not with Devlin looking at me like I'm the most precious thing he's ever seen.

"You're beautiful," he murmurs, his hands reverently tracing the curves of my body. "So goddamn beautiful."

I arch into his touch, my head falling back as his mouth finds the sensitive spot where my neck meets my shoulder. "Devlin," I gasp as his hands and lips continue their exploration, turning me molten from the inside out.

When I can't take it anymore, I reach between us, guiding him where I need him most. We both moan as our bodies join, his cock pressing inside me.

"Look at me," he commands softly, and I open my eyes to find him watching me with an intensity that steals my breath. "I need you to know something."

I still, my heart pounding, waiting.

"I love you too," he says, the words simple but profound. "God help me, but I do, and it scares the hell out of me, because I know Noah and Richard will use it against me. Use you against me."

I roll my hips slowly, savoring the way his breath catches. "Let them try," I whisper fiercely. "They can't break what we're building together."

His hands find my hips again, guiding my movements as we find a rhythm together. "You don't know them," he warns, even as his body responds to mine. "They're powerful men with a lot to lose."

"So are we," I remind him, leaning forward to kiss him deeply. "We have each other. That's more powerful than anything they can throw at us."

He doesn't argue further, giving himself over to the moment, to us. Our bodies move together on the wooden rocking chair, the motion creating a gentle sway that enhances every sensation. I lose myself in him, in the feel of his hands on my skin, his lips on mine, the way he fills me so completely.

When the tension finally breaks, I have to bury my face in his shoulder to muffle my cries. He follows right behind, his arms tightening around me as he shudders beneath me, my name a whisper on his lips.

We stay like that for a long time, tangled together, our breathing gradually slowing, my head resting on his shoulder. The night has grown colder, but I'm warm in his embrace, content in a way I've never known before.

"We should head inside," he eventually murmurs, pressing a kiss to my temple. "Get you warmed up properly."

I nod and reluctantly disentangle myself from him. We gather our scattered clothing, helping each other dress with lingering touches and soft kisses, neither of us quite ready to break the connection between us.

As we head toward the door, Devlin suddenly stops, turning to me with a serious expression. "Atlee, I meant what I said. I love you. But I'm worried that all this"—he gestures vaguely, encompassing the situation with Noah and the Morrisons—"is going to put too much pressure on us. On what we've found."

I reach up, tracing the worry lines between his brows. "I know you're scared," I tell him gently. "I am too. But I meant what I said too. I love you, and I'm not going anywhere. Whatever happens, we face it together."

He catches my hand, pressing a kiss to my palm. "Together," he echoes, but I can still see the shadow of doubt in his eyes, the fear that our newfound happiness might be too fragile to withstand the storm that's coming.

As we step inside, I make a silent promise to myself, to him, to us. I won't let that fear come true. We've both spent too long searching for what we've found in each other to lose it now. No matter what Noah Sanchez or Richard Morrison throw at us, they won't tear us apart.

Some things are worth fighting for, and what Devlin and I have? That's worth everything.

SIXTEEN
DEVLIN

THE NEXT MORNING, I follow Atlee into town, but while she drives over to the pharmacy, I turn down a side street and head toward the Law Offices of Shawn Cooper. True to her word, Atlee spoke to Lennon, and I'm meeting with Shawn Cooper himself today to see what we can do.

I park next to the curb and get out, heading up the walkway. Before I get there, Lennon comes out of the building.

"Hey, I wanted to talk to you before you met with Shawn," she says, putting her hands on her hips and staring at me like she can see right through me.

"All right," I answer, crossing my arms over my chest and rocking back on my heels. "Why do I get the feeling that you're going to make sure your sister is okay? And you're going to do it by making me wish I had one of my brothers to back me up?"

She smirks, running her tongue over her teeth. "I just want to make sure she's okay. If Noah's after her, then I want to make sure she's being protected."

I can sympathize, but there's a part of me that hates that she's having to ask. "No one is going to touch her, I promise. Which is why I'm here to talk to Shawn."

She presses her lips together, and it's like she wants to say something, but instead she nods. "All right. Let me show you inside."

I follow her through the door, taking in the tastefully decorated reception area. It's professional without being pretentious, with leather chairs, dark wood, and framed degrees that let you know Shawn Cooper is the real deal. The receptionist smiles at Lennon and gives me a curious once-over.

"Mr. Cooper is expecting you," she says, gesturing toward a hallway. "Last door on the right."

Lennon leads the way, her heels clicking on the hardwood floors. I've never been much for offices like this. Give me open spaces and the smell of hay and horses any day. But right now, this place might be the only thing standing between me and a jail cell. Between us and losing everything we've built.

"He knows the basics," Lennon says quietly as we walk. "I filled him in on what Atlee told me. But he's going to want to hear everything directly from you." She stops outside a closed door, turning to face me. "And Devlin? He's the best attorney in three counties. If anyone can help you, it's Shawn."

I nod, appreciating her vote of confidence even as anxiety tightens my gut. "Thanks for setting this up."

"I'm not doing it for you," she says bluntly. "I'm doing it for Atlee."

"I know," I acknowledge. "But I appreciate it all the same."

She gives a short nod and knocks on the door. A deep voice calls for us to enter.

Shawn Cooper rises from behind his desk as we walk in. He's older than I expected, maybe mid-fifties, with salt-and-pepper hair and the kind of weathered face that comes from spending time outdoors. Not your typical sits-behind-the-desk lawyer.

"Mr. Nelson," he greets me, extending his hand. His grip is firm, matching my own. "Shawn Cooper. I've been looking forward to meeting you."

"Likewise," I respond, though it's not entirely true. I've been dreading this meeting, dreading having to lay out all our mistakes to a stranger.

"Lennon, would you give us some privacy?" Shawn asks, his tone making it clear it's not really a question.

She hesitates, glancing between us. "Of course," she finally says. "I'll be at my desk if you need anything."

Once the door closes behind her, Shawn gestures for me to take a seat in one of the leather chairs facing his desk. He doesn't return to his own chair but instead takes the one next to mine, removing the barrier between us.

"So," he begins, leaning forward slightly. "I've been briefed on the situation with both Dark Skies Ranch and Grizzly River Ranch. Jesse and Truett were here earlier this morning."

This surprises me. "They were?"

"At my request," Shawn confirms. "I wanted to hear from all parties involved before formulating a strategy. They gave me quite an earful about your cattle rustling operation."

I tense at the direct reference. "Former operation," I correct, uncomfortable with how easily he throws the words around. "We shut it down."

"So I heard," he says, studying me with keen eyes. "But that doesn't erase what's already been done, does it?"

"No," I admit, forcing myself to meet his gaze. "It doesn't."

He nods, seemingly satisfied with my response. "Your brother and Truett filled me in on most of the details, but I'd like to hear your perspective, particularly on what's happening with Deputy Sanchez and Richard Morrison."

I take a deep breath, organizing my thoughts. "Noah has had it in for us since high school. Old grudges...I stole his girlfriend. But this thing with Morrison is different. It's calculated." I explain about Carson hacking into Noah's files, the evidence they've been gathering against us, and the doorbell cameras and traffic footage they've collected.

"Carson found video from a doorbell camera near the Morrison Ranch," I tell him. "Shows our truck driving by on the night we hit their south pasture, and there's traffic camera footage from later that same night. You can see the truck and the livestock trailer, but the license plate isn't visible."

Shawn makes notes on a yellow legal pad as I speak. "And what else did Carson find?"

"A complaint from Richard Morrison claiming he shot one of the rustlers that night." I remember the bullet that almost ended Truett's life, how close we came to disaster. "And there are notes about Noah putting pressure on Atlee, thinking she'll be the one to break and give him what he needs to nail us."

Shawn's pen pauses. "How's Atlee handling all this?"

"Better than I have any right to expect," I admit. "She knows everything, and she's still standing by me. By us."

Something in his expression softens slightly. "Lennon said as much. The Walsh girls have always been fighters."

"Yeah," I agree, thinking of Atlee's strength, her determination. "They have."

Shawn sets his pen down and leans back in his chair. "Here's what you need to know, Devlin. There's an investigation happening at the sheriff's department, and Noah Sanchez is at the center of it."

This catches me off guard. "What kind of investigation?"

"The kind that could end his career," Shawn says bluntly. "Allegations of evidence tampering, witness intimidation, improper relationships with certain prominent citizens... including Richard Morrison."

My mind races with the implications. "So whatever he has against us..."

"He may not bring it out in the open right now," Shawn finishes for me. "He's biding his time, waiting to see how the internal investigation plays out before making any moves against you. Which gives us a window of opportunity."

"How long of a window?" I ask, restless energy making it hard to sit still. "I'm not good at just sitting back and waiting for things to happen."

Shawn's mouth quirks in what might be the ghost of a smile. "So I've heard. But in this case, patience may be your best strategy. The higher-ups in the department are watching Noah carefully. Once everything comes out, and it will come out, he's not going to have a position in the sheriff's office anymore. Any case he's built, any evidence he's gathered, will automatically be called into question."

It sounds too good to be true. "And we just wait?"

"Not exactly," Shawn corrects. "We prepare. We gather our own information on Project Watershed, on Morrison's land grabs, and on Noah's involvement. We build a counter-case that makes any move against you look like retaliation."

"And if Noah moves before the investigation concludes?" The possibility hangs heavy in the air.

"Then we're ready," Shawn assures me. "We've got the groundwork laid for a defense that centers around Morrison's improper influence over law enforcement and his attempts to pressure local ranchers into selling their land. We shift the narrative."

I consider his words, weighing them against my instinct to take action now. "I don't know how long we can wait," I finally say. "Noah's already targeting Atlee, and Morrison is involved. It feels like the noose is tightening."

Shawn leans forward, his expression serious. "Listen to me, Devlin. I understand the impulse to act, to confront this head-on. But sometimes the smartest move is to let your enemies make the first mistake. Noah and Morrison are both under scrutiny. Push them now, and you might give them exactly what they need to justify moving against you."

I run a hand through my hair, frustrated but recognizing the logic in his argument. "All right," I concede. "We play it your way. For now."

"Good," he says, standing and extending his hand again. "Keep your head down, keep in touch with me about any developments, and try not to give Noah any reason to accelerate his timeline."

I rise and shake his hand. "Thanks for meeting with me. For taking this on."

"Thank Lennon," he says. "She's quite adamant about protecting her sister and, by extension, you. But I would've taken the case regardless. Morrison's been throwing his weight around this county for too long. It's time someone pushed back."

As I leave his office, Lennon is waiting in the hallway, arms crossed, expression expectant. "Well?" she demands.

"Your boss thinks we should wait," I tell her. "Let the investigation into Noah play out before making any moves."

She studies my face. "And you don't agree."

It's not a question. "I don't like leaving things to chance," I admit. "Especially when Atlee is involved."

Lennon's expression softens marginally. "Shawn knows what he's doing, Devlin. If he says wait, that's probably your best play."

"Yeah, that's what he said too." I glance at my watch. "I should go. Need to fill the guys in on what's happening."

"Tell my sister I'll call her later," Lennon says as she walks me to the door. "And Devlin? Don't do anything stupid."

I can't help the half-smile that curves my lips. "No promises."

Outside, I slide behind the wheel of my truck but don't start the engine right away. Instead, I sit there, letting Shawn's information sink in. Noah is under investigation. That changes the equation, giving us breathing room we didn't know we had. But it doesn't eliminate the threat.

Morrison is still out there, still pulling strings, and he has a personal grudge against us now, one that goes beyond business. We stole from him, embarrassed him. Men like Richard Morrison don't let that go easily.

I start the truck and head toward Grizzly River Ranch, my mind working through various scenarios. Playing the waiting game might be the smart move legally, but it doesn't sit right with me. In the military, I learned that sometimes the best defense is a good offense. Strike first, set the terms of engagement.

But this isn't a battlefield, and Atlee isn't a soldier. She's the woman I love, the future I never thought I'd have, and that changes everything.

By the time I pull up to the ranch, I've made my decision. We'll follow Shawn's advice for now. We'll wait, we'll watch, we'll gather information. But we'll also be ready to move at the first sign that Noah or Morrison is making a play against us.

Jesse and Truett are waiting on the porch of the main house, with Carson leaning against a support column nearby. They straighten as I approach, eagerness and anxiety written across their faces.

"What's the word?" Jesse asks as soon as I'm within earshot.

I take a deep breath, steeling myself for what's sure to be a heated discussion. "We wait," I tell them, climbing the steps to join them on the porch. "But not for long."

As I explain what Shawn told me, I can see the conflict in their expressions, the same wariness about waiting that I feel, mixed with the hope that Noah's own troubles might save us from ours.

"So we just sit on our hands?" Truett questions, disbelief in his voice. "While Noah and Morrison plot against us?"

"Not exactly," I counter. "We wait for the right moment, and in the meantime, we prepare. Carson, I need you to find out everything you can about this Project Watershed. If Morrison is trying to control the water rights in the county, there must be records, permits, applications."

Carson nods, already looking thoughtful. "I can do that.

Might take some digging, but if it's in any public system, I can find it."

"Good," I say, turning to Jesse and Truett. "You two need to talk to the other local ranchers. Quietly. Find out if Morrison has approached any of them about selling their land and if they've had any run-ins with Noah."

"What are you going to do?" Jesse asks, a knowing look in his eye.

"I'm going to keep Atlee safe," I say firmly. "And I'm going to make sure Noah knows we're not intimidated. We're not running, and we're not hiding."

Truett grins, the first real smile I've seen from him in days. "Now that sounds more like the Devlin Nelson I know."

I don't return the smile. "Just remember, we're playing this smart. No confrontations, no accusations. We gather information, we build our case, and we wait for them to make a mistake."

"And if they don't?" Jesse asks the question we're all thinking.

"Then we reevaluate," I say simply. "One way or another, this ends on our terms, not theirs."

As we break up to begin our assignments, I can't shake the feeling that we're entering the calm before the storm. Noah may be biding his time, but men like him don't give up easily, and Morrison has too much at stake to back down now.

Whatever comes next, I'm ready for it. For the ranch, for my family, for Atlee. I'll do whatever it takes to protect what's mine. That's a promise I intend to keep, no matter what it costs me.

SEVENTEEN
ATLEE

NO MATTER what's going on with Devlin and his brothers, I'm spending the night with my sister. It's been way too long, and maybe it'll do me some good to be away from Devlin for a night. We've possibly been too close, too fast, even though I'm texting him right now.

> **Me**
> What are you planning on doing tonight?

> **Devlin**
> We're playing poker and drinking bourbon.

> **Me**
> Are you heading home tonight afterward?

Devlin
No, we're doing it at Grizzly River, and I'm hoping that I'm too drunk to miss you sleeping next to me, so I'm going to stay with Jesse and Aubree.

Those words send warmth to my chest.

Me
Don't miss me too much.

Devlin
Babe, I'm gonna miss the hell outta you.

That endearment is enough to send a thrill through my stomach. I roll my eyes because of how hot he is when he's not even trying to be, and quickly text him back.

Me
You'll be fine, but I'll miss you, too. I'm heading over to Lennon's now.

Devlin
Be careful, love you.

Every time he tells me those words, I can't believe this is the life I'm living, that someone I love loves me back.

Me
Love you, too.

Three hours later, Lennon and I have polished off a few drinks, eaten way too much spaghetti, and we're laughing as we lie on her couch.

"Why don't you tell me what's up with you and Carson?" I give her a wink. "I didn't know anything was going on with the two of you."

She sighs heavily, taking a drink. "That's because there's absolutely nothing going on between the two of us."

"You're lying. You're lying so hard. The question is, why are you lying?" I take a drink from my beer bottle and tip it toward her.

"Okayyyy." She rolls her eyes, stretching the word out. "Carson came to the office a few months ago. He talked with Shawn, and I can't tell you what it was about, but I had to fill out paperwork for him. We had to talk to one another in order for me to do that, and he flirted with me."

"Flirted?" I question, wanting to know what happened.

"Yeah, he was charming and asked me out..."

I blurt out. "Did you go?"

"Yeah, but he stood me up." She frowns, turning over onto her stomach. "And since then, he's tried to get me to talk to him again, but it hurt my feelings."

I wonder if he stood her up because they were rustling cattle, but I don't say anything. "Would it be so bad if you gave him another shot?"

She cuts her eyes at me. "You know how we grew up, Atlee. We were always promised shit, but it was a lie. Our parents didn't understand that they really needed to keep up with the promises they made."

I understand what she's saying. We've both been left scarred by our childhoods, but sometimes you have to make an exception to your rules. "Do you think you'd like him if you gave him a chance?"

"I don't know." She blows out a breath, her bangs moving. "Maybe that's what I'm actually scared of."

I sit up, tucking my legs beneath me as I consider my sister. We're so different in some ways. She's cautious, where I'm impulsive. She's logical, where I follow my heart. But we share the same scars, the same history of disappointment and broken promises.

"You know," I say carefully, swirling the beer in my bottle. "You could be missing out on something amazing if you don't at least open your heart a little."

Lennon snorts. "Says the girl who fell head over heels for a man in what? Two weeks?"

"I'm serious, Len," I persist, ignoring her jab. "What if Carson is the one person who could actually get past all those walls you've built?"

"What if he's not?" she counters, sitting up to face me. "What if I let him in and he just becomes another person who doesn't show up when I need him?"

There's real pain in her voice, and it hits me in the chest. I reach out, taking her hand in mine. "Then you pick yourself up and try again. Like we always have."

"I'm tired of trying again," she admits, her voice softer now. "I'm tired of believing people when they say they'll be there and then finding myself alone anyway."

I squeeze her hand. "Carson might have had a good reason for standing you up that night."

She eyes me suspiciously. "Do you know something I don't?"

I choose my words carefully, not wanting to give away anything about what the guys were doing. "I just think there's more to him than maybe you're giving him credit for. He seems genuinely interested in you."

"At the bar the other night, you mean?" She takes another sip of her beer. "That was just flirting. It doesn't mean anything."

"Didn't look like 'just flirting' to me," I argue. "The way he looks at you, Len, it's like he's trying to figure you out. Like you're a puzzle he wants to solve."

"Great," she mutters. "Just what I want to be. A puzzle."

"You know what I mean," I sigh, exasperated. "I saw the way you responded to him too. You light up around him. When was the last time anyone made you feel that way?"

She's quiet for a moment, considering. "Mark, maybe. But look how that turned out."

"Not every guy is Mark," I remind her gently. "And you can't judge every potential relationship by the failures of the past ones."

Lennon leans back against the couch cushions, staring up at the ceiling. "That's easy for you to say. You found a good one on your first try."

I can't help but laugh at that. "First try? Have you forgotten about Jake Peterson? Or Tyler from college? Or that disastrous date with the guy from the coffee shop?"

"Okay, point taken," she concedes with a small smile. "But still, what you and Devlin have, it happened so fast, and it seems so solid already. That's not normal, Atlee."

"Maybe not," I acknowledge. "But it's real, and I almost missed out on it because I was scared."

"Scared?" She looks surprised. "You've never been scared of anything."

"That's not true, and you know it," I counter. "I was terrified of getting involved with Devlin at first. He seemed so intense, so...much. But taking that risk was the best decision I ever made."

Lennon studies me for a long moment. "You really love him, don't you?"

"I do," I say simply. "And I can't help thinking that maybe you're missing out on that same feeling because you're too afraid to take a chance."

"It's not just fear," she insists. "It's self-preservation. You know what happened with Mom and Dad. The way they tore each other apart. What if that's our inheritance? What if we're just wired to pick the wrong people, to turn love into something toxic?"

I shake my head firmly. "That's not our inheritance, Len. We're not our parents. We never have been."

"But—"

"No buts," I cut her off. "Look at us. Look at what we've made of ourselves despite everything they did. You're a successful paralegal working for one of the best attorneys in the state. I'm a licensed pharmacist. We have our own places, our own lives. We broke the cycle."

She doesn't look convinced. "In some ways, maybe."

"In all the ways that matter," I insist. "And you could be letting the love of your life slip away because you're still letting Mom and Dad's mistakes define what you think is possible for yourself."

Lennon throws a pillow at me, but there's no real heat behind it. "Since when did you get so wise?"

"Since I let myself fall in love with a complicated man who makes me happier than I ever thought possible," I reply honestly. "It changes your perspective."

She's quiet for a moment, picking at the label on her beer bottle. "What if I'm just not meant to be with anyone? What if some people are just supposed to be alone?"

The sadness in her voice breaks my heart a little. "Do you really believe that?"

"Sometimes," she admits. "Not everyone gets a happy ending, Atlee. Some of us are supporting characters in other people's love stories."

"That's bullshit," I say firmly. "You're the main character in your own story, Len. Always have been. And there's no reason you can't have what I have with Devlin, or something even better that works for you."

"Maybe," she says, but I can tell she's not convinced.

"Just promise me you'll think about giving Carson another chance if he asks again," I urge. "Just one real date. If it's terrible, I'll never bring it up again."

She sighs dramatically. "If it'll get you off my back, fine. One date. *If* he asks again. Which he probably won't."

"He will," I say confidently. "I've seen the way he looks at you."

"Whatever," she mumbles, but I catch the faint smile tugging at her lips.

We lapse into comfortable silence for a while, the TV playing softly in the background. It's nice just being here with her like old times, before Devlin, before the robbery.

"So," Lennon finally says, breaking the silence. "You think you and Devlin are in it for the long haul?"

The question catches me off guard. "I hope so," I answer honestly. "I've never felt this way about anyone before."

"Even with all the drama?" she asks pointedly. "The stuff with Noah and the Morrisons?"

I tense slightly, wondering how much she knows. "What do you mean?"

She gives me a look that says she's not buying my innocent act. "Atlee, I work for Shawn Cooper. I've seen Devlin, Jesse, and Truett coming in and out of the office. I don't know exactly what's going on, but I know it's serious."

I take a deep breath, deciding how much to reveal. "It's complicated," I finally say. "But yes, even with all that. Maybe especially with all that. It's easy to be with someone when everything's perfect. The real test is standing by them when things get hard."

"And you're ready for that? Whatever comes next?"

"I am," I say without hesitation. "He's worth it. We're worth it."

Lennon studies me, then nods slowly. "Then I'm happy for you. And I've got your back, whatever happens. You know that, right?"

"I know," I say, warmth spreading through my chest at her words. "And I've got yours too. Always."

She yawns, stretching her arms over her head. "God, I'm tired. And maybe a little drunk."

I laugh, feeling the pleasant buzz of alcohol myself. "Same. We should probably get some sleep."

Lennon gets up, swaying slightly as she heads to her linen

closet to grab blankets and pillows for the pull-out couch. "You good out here?"

"Perfect," I assure her, helping her set up the makeshift bed.

Once we've got everything arranged, she pauses in the doorway of her bedroom. "Hey, Atlee?"

"Yeah?"

"Thank you," she says softly. "For pushing me about Carson. I don't know if anything will ever happen there, but...it's nice to know you believe I deserve something good."

"You do," I tell her earnestly. "You deserve everything good, Len."

She smiles, a real smile that reaches her eyes. "So do you. Good night, sis."

"Good night," I reply, watching as she disappears into her room.

As I settle onto the pull-out couch, my phone buzzes with a text from Devlin.

Devlin
Miss you. Jesse is cheating at poker and I'm down $50.

I smile, typing back quickly.

Me
Miss you too. And he's definitely cheating. Watch his left hand. I've heard rumors about that being his tell.

Devlin
Thanks for the tip. How's your night with Lennon?

Me
Good. Talked about Carson actually.

Devlin
Oh yeah? Anything I should tell him?

I think about Lennon's reluctant promise.

Me
Maybe. I'll fill you in tomorrow. Go back to your game. Love you.

Devlin
Love you too. Sleep well.

I set my phone aside and snuggle down under the blankets, my thoughts drifting between Devlin and Lennon. I hope my sister will give Carson a chance. I hope she'll open herself up to the possibility of finding what Devlin and I have found.

Not everyone believes in love stories with happy endings. Lennon has always been more pragmatic than I am and more guarded with her heart. But I've seen the way her eyes light up when Carson is around. I've seen the spark that she tries so hard to deny.

As I drift off to sleep, I find myself hoping that my sister is wrong, that she's not meant to be alone, that there's someone out there for her too. Maybe it's Carson, maybe it's someone we haven't even met yet. But everyone deserves a chance at the kind of happiness I've found with Devlin, especially Lennon.

And if there's one thing the Walsh sisters know how to do, it's fight for what we want. Even if sometimes the hardest fight is against our own fears.

EIGHTEEN DEVLIN

WAKING up without Atlee isn't my favorite thing to do. I missed the hell out of her last night, but I know it's important that she has time with her sister, just like it's important for me to have time with my brothers where we aren't stressing over Noah and Richard.

Glancing at the clock, it's way too early to be up after drinking the night before, but I know I'm not going to be able to sleep any longer. Going into the kitchen, I greet Cookie. "Morning."

"Morning to you too. Are you staying for breakfast?"

"Nah, I think I'm heading home after I grab some coffee. There are a few things I wanted to get done today."

I've been thinking about building a couple of shelving units so that Atlee has a place to put her stuff when I ask her to move in with me. I just hope she says yes.

Cookie nods and pours hot liquid into a to-go cup. "Fix it up however you want it."

"Prefer it black. Thank you." I tip the cup to him.

"Not a problem. I'll let everyone know that you left if you want me to?"

I nod and take a healthy drink. "Appreciate it, Cookie. See ya later."

Walking out to my truck, I shiver, realizing I should've brought my jacket. I get in and wait for the engine to warm up enough for me to leave.

The drive home is peaceful, the kind of quiet that settles into your bones. The sun is just starting to peek over the mountains, painting the sky in shades of gold and pink. It's the kind of morning that reminds me why I came back to Grizzly River, why this place will always be home no matter how far I roam.

As I turn down the long driveway that leads to my cabin, something in my chest loosens. There it is, my place. Not grand like the main house, not fancy by any stretch, but mine. Built with my own two hands, every board and design was my own choice, with no one telling me when I had to do things, or that they had to be a certain way. It's been my expression of creativity since I started working on it.

I pull up to the cabin and sit for a moment, just looking at it. When I came back from the military, I was a mess. Nightmares kept me up at night, and the smallest sounds would set me off. I needed space, needed walls that belonged only to me, a place where I could breathe without feeling like I was being watched or judged.

Jesse understood, even if he didn't like it. He gave me this little parcel of land without question, helped me clear it, and then stepped back and let me do the rest on my own. I designed this place to be a sanctuary, somewhere quiet where I could put myself back together.

Never once did I think it would become a home for two.

But now I can't imagine it any other way. Atlee fits here like she was always meant to be part of it. Her laughter fills the empty corners, and her scent mingles with the cedar and pine. It's not just my sanctuary anymore. It's ours.

I grab my coffee and head inside, letting the familiar smells wash over me. The wood from the walls, the spice of the candles that Atlee likes to burn—it smells like home in a way it never did when it was just me.

Setting my coffee on the counter, I head to the spare room where I keep my tools. I've got most of what I need for the shelving units, and what I don't have, I can improvise. I've been doing that my whole life.

I haul the lumber I'd stashed in there out to the living room, lay it all out on the floor, and start taking measurements. I want to make sure these shelves fit perfectly in the bedroom, right next to the closet. Someplace Atlee can put all those little bottles and jars women seem to collect, plus room for whatever else she wants to bring over.

If she says yes, that is.

The thought of her saying no makes my hands still for a moment. What if she thinks it's too soon? What if she's not ready to give up her independence? What if...

I shake my head, forcing the doubts away. Can't live life asking "what if." If there's one thing the military taught me, it's that you make your move and deal with the consequences as they come. No use worrying about things you can't control.

Besides, she loves me. She told me so herself, right out there on the back porch under the stars, and I believe her. I have to believe her, because the alternative is unthinkable.

I work steadily through the morning, measuring twice, cutting once, just like my dad taught me. The physical labor feels good, keeps my mind focused on something other than Noah and Morrison and all the shit hanging over our heads. For a few hours, I can just be a man building something for the woman he loves.

By early afternoon, I've got the main frames built for both units. Five shelves each, solid pine that'll last for years. I just need to sand them down, stain them to match the bedroom furniture, and mount them on the wall. Not bad for a day's work.

I'm so caught up in sanding the rough edges that I don't hear the car pulling up outside. The front door opens, and I look up to see Atlee standing there, a smile spreading across her face as she takes in the mess I've made of our living room.

"What's all this?" she asks, setting her bag down by the door and picking her way through the sawdust and wood scraps to reach me.

I set aside the sandpaper, suddenly feeling a little self-conscious. "Just doing some upgrades to the cabin."

She raises an eyebrow, surveying the half-finished shelving units. "Looks like more than just some upgrades to me."

I rub the back of my neck, sawdust falling from my hair. "Yeah, well...I thought it was time to make some changes around here."

She comes closer, running her fingers along the smooth wood of one of the frames. "What kind of changes?"

This is it. The moment I've been building toward all day.

My heart hammers against my ribs, but I force myself to meet her gaze.

"Shelving units," I say, trying to sound casual. "Figured you'd need somewhere to put your stuff if...if you decided to move in. Permanently, I mean."

Her hand stills on the wood, her eyes widening slightly. "Are you asking me to move in with you? Like, officially?"

I swallow hard, nodding. "Yeah, I am. I know it's fast, and I know with everything going on with Noah and Morrison, the timing might not be ideal, but...I want this, Atlee. I want you here with me. Every day."

She's quiet for a moment, her expression unreadable, and my stomach drops. Shit. It is too soon. I've pushed too hard, too fast.

But then her face breaks into the most radiant smile I've ever seen. "Yes!" she screams, launching herself at me.

I barely have time to open my arms before she's there, legs wrapping around my waist, arms around my neck. I stagger back a step from the impact but hold her tight, her weight solid in my arms.

"Yes, yes, yes," she says between kisses, her lips finding mine, my cheek, my jaw, anywhere she can reach. "Of course I'll move in with you."

Relief floods through me, so intense it's almost painful. I bury my face in her neck, breathing her in, this woman who's become my whole world in such a short time.

"I love you," I whisper against her skin. "God, Atlee, I love you so much."

She pulls back just enough to look at me, her eyes bright with unshed tears. "I love you too, Devlin. More than I ever thought possible."

I carry her over to the couch, carefully navigating around the lumber and tools scattered across the floor. We sink down together, her still in my lap, neither of us willing to let go just yet.

"I missed you last night," I tell her, tucking a strand of hair behind her ear.

"I missed you too," she admits, her fingers playing with the hair at the nape of my neck. "Lennon's pull-out couch has nothing on sleeping next to you."

I laugh softly. "Glad to hear it."

She glances over at the shelving units, a smile playing at the corners of her mouth. "So you built those for me? Today?"

"Started them," I correct her. "Still need to finish sanding and staining them, then mount them on the wall."

"I can't believe you did all this," she says, wonder in her voice. "Built these with your own hands, just for me."

I shrug, a little embarrassed by her obvious admiration. "It's not a big deal. Just wanted you to have space for your things."

"It is a big deal," she insists. "No one's ever...no one's ever made room for me like this before."

The vulnerability in her voice hits me right in the chest. I know enough about her childhood to understand what she's really saying. No one's ever wanted her enough to build something just for her, to carve out space in their life specifically with her in mind.

"Well, get used to it," I tell her, trying to keep my tone light despite the emotion swelling in my throat. "Because I plan on making room for you in every part of my life, for as long as you'll have me."

Her eyes soften. "That might be a very long time, Devlin Nelson."

"I'm counting on it," I say, pulling her closer for a kiss.

She responds eagerly, her body melting against mine, her hands sliding into my hair. I lose myself in her—the softness of her lips, the sweet scent of her skin, the little sounds she makes in the back of her throat when I deepen the kiss.

When we finally break apart, both breathing harder, she rests her forehead against mine. "When can I start moving my things over?"

"Whenever you want," I tell her. "Tomorrow, next week... hell, we could go get some of your stuff right now if you're that eager."

She laughs. "I kind of am. Is that pathetic?"

"Not at all," I assure her, dropping a kiss on the tip of her nose. "It's exactly how I feel too."

She snuggles closer, her head finding that perfect spot on my shoulder like it was made to fit there. "I should probably give notice at my apartment. And figure out what to do with my furniture."

"We can store anything you want to keep," I offer. "Or sell it, donate it. Whatever you want."

"I don't need much," she says thoughtfully. "Most of it was just temporary stuff anyway. Things to fill the space until I found something that I really liked. A lot of it was from thrift stores, and I paid next to nothing for it."

The simplicity of her statement hits me hard. That's exactly what this cabin was for me too—a temporary sanctuary, a place to heal and hide until I figured out what came next. Neither of us realized that what came next would be each other.

"We can take our time," I tell her, running my hand up and

down her spine. "No rush. You can bring over whatever makes this feel like home to you."

She lifts her head, looking around the cabin with new eyes. "It already feels like home," she says softly. "Because you're here."

Something fierce and protective swells in my chest. Whatever happens with Noah and Morrison, whatever trouble comes our way, I will keep this woman safe. I will protect what we've built together—this fragile, beautiful thing that somehow sprouted in the ruins of both our pasts.

"I was thinking," I say, threading my fingers through hers. "Maybe we could fix up the back porch a bit more. Add some string lights, maybe a swing for the summer."

Her whole face lights up at the suggestion. "I'd love that."

"And maybe we could plant some flowers come spring," I continue, warming to the idea of building a future with her, project by project. "Or even a small vegetable garden, if you're interested in that sort of thing."

"I've always wanted to grow tomatoes," she admits, a shy smile playing at her lips. "And maybe some herbs for cooking."

"Then that's what we'll do," I promise her. "This place is ours now, Atlee. We can make it whatever we want it to be."

She kisses me then, soft and sweet, full of promise. "Our home," she whispers against my lips. "I like the sound of that."

"Me too," I whisper back, holding her close, this woman who's somehow become my future, my heart, my everything.

Outside, the world keeps turning. Noah and Morrison are still out there, still plotting. Our troubles aren't over. But in this moment, with Atlee in my arms and plans for our future taking shape between us, none of that seems to matter quite as much.

We've found something worth fighting for. I'll be damned if anyone rips it from me.

NINETEEN
ATLEE

I'VE SPENT most of the day watching Devlin build the shelving units for me. There's something about watching the man you love use his hands to make a piece of furniture for you. It's one of the hottest things I've seen. Lying on the couch, I watch him, and since we have all this time together, I decide to ask a few questions.

"What happened to you and Noah Sanchez's girlfriend? Did you really steal her away from him in high school?"

He gives me a smirk, his eyebrows raising as he bends over and makes a cut on one of his pieces of wood. "Yeah, I did, but there's more to it than that. He was a dickhead to her, and both of us were on the football team. He was the quarterback, and I was the tight end. I saw what he was doing to her."

"And what was that?" I ask, putting my chin in my palm, giving him my full attention.

His face goes hard, and I wonder if this is what it looked like when he was performing a mission in the military. "He was a bully, even back then. One night, I was out with some friends, and when I was driving home, I saw her walking on the side of the road."

"Why was she walking?" I ask, my stomach clenching because I have a feeling I know why, but it's horrible, so I don't want to give voice to it.

Devlin sets down his tools, wiping sawdust from his hands onto his jeans. The playful mood from earlier has evaporated, replaced by one that's decidedly heavier and darker.

"Her name was Jessalyn," he says, leaning against the workbench he's created in the middle of our living room. "She was walking because Noah had kicked her out of his truck after some party. It was about two miles outside of town, pitch black, middle of nowhere."

My heart sinks. "That's awful."

"That's not even the worst part," Devlin continues, his voice tight with controlled anger. "When I pulled over to see if she needed help, I could see she'd been hit. Hard. Across the face. Her cheek was swollen, her lip split. Her shirt was ripped too."

I sit up straighter on the couch, my hands curling into fists without me even realizing it. "Noah did that to her?"

Devlin nods, his jaw clenched. "Yeah. Apparently, they'd been arguing about something—she never did tell me exactly what—and he just...snapped. Hit her, ripped her shirt trying to grab her when she tried to get away, then dumped her on the side of the road when she wouldn't stop crying. Keep in mind this is him as a teenager, not the adult cop he is now with more power."

"Jesus," I breathe. I knew Noah was dangerous, but I don't like hearing something like this.

"I gave her my jacket and drove her home," Devlin continues. "Made sure she got inside safe. Gave her my number in case she needed anything else."

"And that's how you two started..." I trail off, letting him fill in the blanks.

He runs a hand through his hair, scattering more sawdust. "Not right away. She called me a couple of days later, just to thank me. Then we started talking more. She was in my English class, so we'd sit together, study together. Eventually, it turned into us hanging out on the weekends, and then one day I kissed her."

I can picture it—young Devlin, already protective, already drawn to helping someone in trouble. "Did you love her?" The question slips out before I can stop it.

He considers this, his expression thoughtful. "In a way. Not the way I should have, maybe. Not the way I..." He trails off, his eyes finding mine. "We were comfortable together. She was sweet, smart. But it wasn't...it wasn't like this. She deserved more than what I could give her, which is why she didn't wait for me."

The words hang between us, weighted with meaning. *Not like what we have.*

"What happened with Noah?" I ask, already suspecting the answer.

Devlin's mouth curves into something that's not quite a smile. "I waited two weeks. Let Jessalyn heal up and made sure she was okay. Then I caught Noah alone in the locker room after practice."

"And?"

"And I beat the living shit out of him," Devlin says simply, with no pride or regret in his voice, just stating a fact. "Broke his nose, cracked two ribs, left him with a black eye that didn't fade for a month."

I should probably be horrified by the casual way he describes violence, but all I feel is a fierce, savage satisfaction. "Good."

That gets a genuine smile from him, brief but real. "That's not what most people say when they hear that story."

"I'm not most people," I remind him.

"No," he agrees, his eyes warming as they hold mine. "You definitely aren't."

He turns back to his work, measuring a piece of wood with careful precision. "Anyway, that's why Noah's got it in for me—actually, for the whole family. Jesse stood lookout in the locker room. He's been waiting all these years to get back at me. Football scholarship, college plans, his reputation—of it took a hit after what happened. And Noah is the type to hold a grudge."

"Did Jessalyn press charges against him? For what he did to her?" I ask, although knowing that probably didn't happen since he's now a cop.

Devlin shakes his head. "She didn't want to. Said it would just make things worse. It was his word against hers, and things weren't as fair back then? Maybe is a good way to put it. Now, people are more likely to believe a girl. Back then, they weren't."

I do know. In places like Grizzly River, victims often stay silent rather than face the whispers, the judgment, the inevitable taking of sides. It's less so now, but it was definitely that way back then.

"What happened to her? To Jessalyn?" I ask, realizing I've never heard this name around town.

"After we broke up, by letter, I might add..." He chuckles. "She moved out east. Last I heard, she was living in Boston, married with a couple of kids." He smiles faintly. "She sends me a Christmas card every year. Might seem weird, but I'm happy to know she's happy."

The thought of Devlin receiving Christmas cards from an ex-girlfriend would have bothered me a few weeks ago. Now, knowing the full story, it just makes me love him more.

"That's why you stepped in with me, isn't it?" I ask softly. "At the pharmacy. You saw someone else who needed help, and you couldn't walk away."

He looks up from his work, his eyes serious. "I'd have helped anyone in that situation, Atlee. But with you..." He pauses, searching for words. "With you, it was different. Right from the start."

My heart flutters at the intensity in his gaze. "Different how?"

He sets down his tools again, crossing the room to sit beside me on the couch. His hand finds mine, callused fingers twining with my smoother ones.

"With Jessalyn, I wanted to protect her because it was the right thing to do," he explains. "With you, I wanted to protect you because the thought of anything happening to you felt like someone ripping my heart out of my chest. Especially after us having hung out previously. There's been something about you since that first night that I haven't been able to let go."

The raw honesty in his voice steals my breath. I squeeze his hand, unable to find words.

"Noah knows that," Devlin continues. "He's smart enough to see what you mean to me. That's why he's targeting you now."

"You think this is all about revenge?" I ask. "The cattle

rustling, Project Watershed...it's just an excuse to come after you?"

"Not entirely," Devlin admits. "The Morrisons are definitely up to something with the water rights. And we did steal their cattle, so that part's real enough. But Noah wouldn't be pushing so hard if it weren't personal. He's been waiting for his chance, and now he thinks he's got it."

"Because of me," I say quietly.

His eyes flash. "This isn't your fault, Atlee. Not any of it."

"I didn't say it was," I counter. "But I am involved now. Noah sees me as your weakness, as a way to get to you."

"You're not my weakness," Devlin says fiercely. "You're my strength. But yes, he's going to try to use you against me. That's why I'm worried. My life's been complicated enough before you came along, but now..."

"Now what?" I challenge when he doesn't finish.

He sighs, running his free hand over his face. "Now I've got so much more to lose."

I shift on the couch, turning to face him fully. "You are a good man, Devlin Nelson. The way you helped Jessalyn, the way you stood up to Noah...not many people would have done that."

He looks away, uncomfortable with the praise. "I did what anyone would do."

"No," I disagree, reaching up to turn his face back toward mine. "You didn't. Most people would have kept driving, would have told themselves it wasn't their business. But you stopped. You helped. Just like you helped me."

"And look where it's gotten you," he says bitterly. "A target on your back, caught up in all this mess with the Morrisons and Noah."

"I'm exactly where I want to be," I tell him firmly. "Right here, with you."

"Even if it makes you a target?" he asks, a trace of vulnerability in the question.

I lean forward, pressing my lips to his in a gentle kiss. "I would be a target every day," I whisper against his mouth. "If it meant I got to spend every night with you."

He groans softly, his arms coming around me, pulling me closer. "You're too good for me, you know that?"

"I'm exactly right for you," I correct him. "Just like you're exactly right for me."

We stay like that for a long moment, holding each other on the couch, surrounded by half-built shelving units and sawdust. It's not perfect. There's still Noah and the Morrisons to deal with, still a storm brewing on the horizon. But it's real. It's ours.

"I should finish these shelves," Devlin finally says, though he makes no move to let me go.

"They can wait," I tell him, sliding my hands up his chest to link behind his neck. "We've got time."

His eyes darken at my words, his hands tightening on my waist. "Do we?"

"All the time in the world," I assure him, bringing my lips to his again.

And for a little while, at least, I almost believe it. The troubles outside our door fade away, and there's just us, Devlin and Atlee, building something together that no one, not even Noah Sanchez, can tear down.

Later, as the afternoon stretches toward evening and Devlin returns to his woodworking, I find myself thinking about Jessalyn and about how one small act of kindness—stopping to help a girl on a dark road—can change the course of multiple lives. If Devlin hadn't stopped that night, would Noah have become the man he is now? Would Devlin? Would either of them have crossed my path?

It's strange how life works, how the worst moments can lead to the best ones if you just keep going, keep trying, keep believing that there's something better waiting ahead.

As I watch Devlin work, his strong hands crafting something meant to last, I make a silent promise to myself. Whatever comes our way—Noah, the Morrisons, or some new trouble we haven't even imagined yet—we'll face it together, because some things are worth fighting for.

And what Devlin and I have? That's worth everything.

TWENTY
DEVLIN

AFTER SPENDING time with Atlee yesterday, I'm ready for the workday on Monday. I watch as she exits the driveway and turns onto the main road, then I get in my truck and head for the Grizzly River Ranch. When I get there, I see one of my brothers I haven't seen in a while. Getting out of my truck, I walk over. "Where the fuck you been, Austin?"

He gives me a grin. "Doing a little reconnaissance, which is why I'm here today. I'm calling a meeting in the barn."

We're starting to call more meetings than actually get work done, but I'm glad to see my younger brother. It's been way too long. When I get inside, I see the rest of the guys are already there. "Sorry, I seem to be late."

Jesse takes a drink of his coffee. "Truett and I were already out here, and Carson just showed up. You aren't as late as you think you are."

I appreciate that he's willing to give me an out. I have been getting to the ranch later than I used to, but at least I have a good reason. "So what's this I'm hearing about Austin doing reconnaissance?"

Austin pushes his hat off his head and runs his fingers through his hair. "Y'all are about to get arrested, but I need you to go with it. Noah will be here in the next hour. I spent last night meeting with Shawn Cooper, and he knows the deal. Lennon has already started to work on some of the paperwork. So as soon as they ask to speak with you, just say lawyer. Shawn will be waiting for all of you at the jail."

My stomach clenches. I don't do well in spaces or situations where I'm forced to follow rules. Not anymore. I'm just about to say those words when I hear sirens and what sounds like a bunch of cars coming down the driveway.

"That was faster than expected," Austin mutters, glancing toward the barn doors.

"Shit," Carson hisses, looking around like he's searching for an escape route.

Jesse holds up a hand, his expression calm despite the approaching chaos. "Everyone needs to put their hands up and kneel. There's no reason for us to cause a disruption. Let them come in, do what they need to do. If we don't fight, then they have no reason to use force."

Truett looks like he wants to argue, but he catches Jesse's warning glance and nods reluctantly.

I take a deep breath, trying to calm the roaring in my ears. Enclosed spaces, restraints, loss of control—these are the things that trigger the worst of my PTSD episodes. But Jesse is right. Fighting will only make things worse.

"Do what he says," I instruct, already lowering myself to one knee, hands raised above my head.

The others follow suit, forming a line of kneeling men in the center of the barn. Austin stands off to the side, hands also raised but remaining on his feet.

"It'll be okay," he says quietly. "Just follow the plan."

The sirens cut off abruptly, and the sound of car doors slamming echoes through the morning air. Heavy footsteps approach the barn, and then the doors burst open, flooding the dim space with harsh sunlight.

"Sheriff's department! Nobody move!" The shout comes from one of the deputies I don't recognize, his gun drawn and pointed in our general direction.

More officers file in behind him, including Noah, who strides forward with a smug smile playing at the corners of his mouth. He's enjoying this, the power trip of seeing us on our knees with our hands up.

"Well, well," he drawls, coming to stand in front of me. "Devlin Nelson. How the mighty have fallen."

I say nothing, keeping my eyes fixed straight ahead. Any reaction would only feed his ego, giving him the satisfaction he's looking for.

"You're all under arrest for cattle theft, conspiracy, and interfering with a police investigation," Noah announces, loud enough for everyone to hear. He gestures to the other officers. "Cuff 'em."

The deputies move in, pulling our arms behind our backs and securing them with plastic zip ties. One of them is unnecessarily rough with Carson, yanking his arms so hard he winces.

"Easy," Jesse warns, earning himself an extra-tight cinch of his own restraints.

When it's my turn, Noah steps forward. "I'll take this one," he tells the deputy who is approaching me.

I can feel the tension radiating from my brothers as Noah circles behind me, but I give them a slight shake of my head. Don't interfere. We've got a plan.

"You know," Noah says, leaning down close to my ear as he secures the zip ties around my wrists. "I've been waiting for this moment for a long time. Payback for what you did to me."

I remain silent, focusing on my breathing. In through the nose, out through the mouth. The way my old combat instructor taught us to handle stress.

"Nothing to say?" Noah taunts, pulling the restraints so tight they immediately start cutting into my skin. "No smart-ass remarks? No threats?"

When I still don't respond, I see a flash of frustration cross his face. He wants a reaction, something to justify escalating this beyond a simple arrest.

"Get up," he orders, grabbing my arm and hauling me to my feet with unnecessary force.

I comply, rising smoothly despite the awkward position of my arms behind my back. The others are being pulled to their feet as well, all of us maintaining a dignified silence that seems to irritate Noah more by the second.

"Start walking," he commands, shoving me toward the barn door.

As I take a step forward, he sticks his foot out, tripping me. I stumble but manage to catch myself before falling, years of combat training keeping me upright despite the handicap of having my hands bound.

"Stop resisting!" Noah shouts, grabbing the back of my neck and slamming me against one of the support beams of the barn.

"I'm not—" I start to say, but he cuts me off with a backhand across my face, the sharp crack of it echoing through the barn.

"Noah! What the fuck?" Jesse barks, taking a step forward before another deputy restrains him.

I taste blood in my mouth and feel it trickling from the corner of my lips. But instead of anger, a strange calm settles over me. This is exactly what we need—evidence of Noah's corruption, his personal vendetta clouding his professional judgment.

Slowly, I turn my head back to face him, a smile spreading across my bloodied lips. "You might want to save some of that for later," I tell him quietly. "Because once I'm out of these cuffs and past all this legal bullshit, I'll be happy to meet you somewhere private to settle the score."

A flicker of uncertainty passes through his eyes before he masks it with another show of bravado. "Get him out of here," he says to the nearest deputy, stepping back.

They march us out into the yard where three patrol cars and a transport van wait. The morning sun is bright, making me squint as they guide us toward the vehicles. Ranch hands have gathered at a distance, watching with concerned expressions as their bosses are led away in restraints.

"Tell Aubree what's happening," Jesse calls to one of them. "And call Shawn Cooper!" he says, mostly for show. We don't want them to know that he's already on his way because he knows we're getting arrested.

"This sucks," Austin grumbles from behind us. He's being led out too, but his hands aren't bound. He catches my eye and gives me a subtle nod of reassurance. Everything's going according to plan.

They load us into the transport van—Jesse, Truett, Carson and me—while Austin is placed in one of the patrol cars. The ride to the county jail is tense and silent. The plastic restraints dig into my wrists, and my cheek throbs where Noah struck me. But none of that matters. What matters is that Atlee is safe, unaware of what's happening. I hope she stays that way until this is resolved.

The county jail is a squat, gray building on the outskirts of town. They lead us inside through a back entrance, avoiding the public areas where we might be seen. We get booked with mugshots and fingerprints. They keep us separated during this process, but I can hear Carson asking repeatedly to speak with his lawyer, following the script perfectly.

After booking, they place us in a holding cell together, minus Austin, who's been taken elsewhere. The cell is small, designed for temporary holding rather than long-term confinement, with a bench running along three walls and a stainless steel toilet in the corner.

"Well, this is cozy," Truett remarks, rubbing his wrists where the restraints have left angry red marks.

"Everyone okay?" Jesse asks, looking us each over with concern.

Carson nods, though he looks pale and shaken. This is his first arrest, and despite our planning, the reality of it is clearly hitting him hard.

"Fine," I answer, though the ache in my jaw suggests Noah's hit might have done some damage. "Just ready to get this over with."

"It won't be long now," Jesse assures us. "Shawn should be here any minute."

As if on cue, the door to the holding area opens, and a deputy appears. "Your lawyer is here," he announces, sounding less than pleased about it.

We're led to an interview room where Shawn Cooper waits, looking impeccable in a tailored gray suit. Beside him stands Lennon, her blonde hair pulled back in a severe bun, her expression all business.

"Gentlemen," Shawn greets us as we file in. "Please take a seat."

Once the door closes behind the deputy, Shawn's professional demeanor softens slightly. "Well, that happened faster than we anticipated. Austin barely had time to warn everybody before they moved in."

"How bad is it?" Jesse asks, getting straight to the point. "They told us some shit out there, but I have a feeling it's more than what they said."

"They've got warrants for all four of you on charges of cattle rustling, conspiracy, and as a special bonus, obstruction of justice," Shawn explains, opening a folder on the table. "The evidence is largely circumstantial.—the doorbell camera footage Carson discovered, some testimony from Morrison about suspicious vehicles on his property, and what appears to be an anonymous tip about your sudden financial turnaround."

"What about Austin?" I ask. "Why did they bring him in?"

"Material witness," Lennon answers, speaking for the first time. "They're hoping he'll flip on y'all, not knowing he's already working with us."

"Devlin," Shawn says, frowning as he takes in my face. "What happened there?"

I touch my cheek, wincing slightly. "Noah happened. Said I was resisting arrest."

"Was anyone else present when this occurred?" Shawn asks, his eyes sharpening with interest.

"All of us," Jesse confirms. "Plus at least three other deputies."

"Perfect," Shawn says, making a note. "That's exactly the kind of behavior that supports our narrative about Noah's personal vendetta interfering with his professional duties."

Lennon steps forward, her eyes fixed on my injured face. "We'll document that before the arraignment," she says. "It'll help with the harassment claim we're filing."

"Arraignment?" Carson asks, looking confused. "When is that happening?"

"In about an hour," Shawn explains. "Judge Holloway is on the bench today, which is a stroke of luck for us. She's fair and not easily swayed by the Morrison influence."

"What's our play here?" Truett asks.

"Simple," Shawn says. "We acknowledge you've had financial difficulties, acknowledge you've recently come into some money, but maintain the source was legitimate with the land sale. We argue that Noah's evidence is circumstantial at best, tainted by personal bias at worst, and that you're all upstanding members of the community with strong ties to the area, making you low flight risks."

"And if they press about the cattle?" Jesse asks.

"We say nothing about that," Lennon interjects firmly. "Not a word. That's what the Fifth Amendment is for."

Shawn nods in agreement. "The burden of proof is on them. Right now, all they have is conjecture and a grainy video that doesn't clearly identify any of you. It's not enough for a conviction."

"What about bail?" I ask, thinking about Atlee. I need to get back to her before she hears about this from someone else.

"Given the nonviolent nature of the charges and your community ties, we should be able to secure release on bond," Shawn assures me. "It might be substantial, but I'm guessing that won't be a problem given the proceeds from your recent land sale."

There's a knowing look in his eye that tells me he's well aware all our money didn't come from the land sale. But he's smart enough not to ask questions he doesn't want the answers to.

"Any other questions before we head to court?" Shawn asks, gathering his papers.

"Just one," I say quietly. "Has anyone contacted Atlee?"

Lennon's expression softens slightly. "Not yet. I thought it would be better coming from you once you're released."

I nod, grateful for her understanding. "Thank you."

The arraignment is a blur of legal formalities. We stand before Judge Holloway, a stern-faced woman in her sixties with sharp eyes that seem to miss nothing. Shawn presents our case exactly as he outlined, emphasizing our deep roots in the community and the circumstantial nature of the evidence against us.

The prosecutor, a young woman I vaguely recognize as being someone's little sister that I went to school with, argues for remand, citing the serious nature of the charges and the potential flight risk. But her arguments lack conviction, as if she knows she's fighting a losing battle.

Noah stands at the back of the courtroom, his arms crossed over his chest, his expression darkening as the proceedings continue to go our way.

In the end, Judge Holloway sets bond at fifty thousand dollars each. It's a lot, but we can cover it.

"The defendants will surrender their passports and check in weekly with the court until trial," she orders, banging her gavel to signify the end of the hearing.

As we're led out to process the bond payment, I catch sight of Noah in the hallway, his face flushed with anger. Our eyes meet briefly, and I see a promise in his. *This isn't over*.

But for now, we've won the first round. And as I think about getting home to Atlee, explaining what's happened, and reassuring her that everything will be okay, I find myself feeling strangely calm. There are still battles ahead, still a war to be fought against Noah and the Morrisons. But for the first time since this all began, I believe we might actually win it.

Because now we're fighting on our terms, not theirs, and that makes all the difference in the world.

TWENTY-ONE
ATLEE

I'M WAITING outside the jail, biting my nails as I wait for Devlin to come out. The door opens, and out comes Lennon. "Hey," I wave her over. "What's happening in there?"

Lennon grabs my arms, steering me so that I'm leaning against my SUV. "They're getting bonded out. The arraignment went well, and I have a feeling they won't be indicted by the grand jury. The evidence is circumstantial at best, and tomorrow there's going to be an article printed in the Grizzly River Gazette about Project Watershed. Once all the other ranchers know about what Noah and the Morrison family are planning on doing, no one will want to indict them. They'll see it as the guys being bullied because they're fighting against people who want to harm the ranchers."

I feel better hearing her speak. Everything she's saying makes so much sense, but I won't be completely calm until I get Devlin in my arms.

"How long until they're released?" I ask, my eyes darting back to the jail doors.

"Paperwork is being processed now," Lennon says, giving my arm a reassuring squeeze. "Could be fifteen minutes, could be an hour. You know how bureaucracy works."

I don't really know, but I nod, trying to keep my anxiety in check.

"Did you see him? Is he okay?" The questions tumble out before I can stop them.

Lennon's expression changes, a flicker of anger crossing her face. "Noah roughed him up a bit. Split his lip."

My stomach drops. "What? What a fucking asshole."

"Don't worry. We're documenting everything. It's all going to work in our favor when we file the harassment suit."

"I don't care about the lawsuit," I say, my voice rising. "I care about Devlin being hurt!"

She sighs, running a hand through her hair. "I know, sis. I know. But he's tough, you know that, and he's more worried about you than anything else."

That doesn't surprise me. Even now, even when he's the one in trouble, his concern is for me. It's just who he is.

I lean back against my SUV, trying to calm my racing heart. The parking lot of the county jail is nearly empty, just a few official vehicles and Lennon's car beside mine. The coming winter air is crisp, carrying the scent of pine from the surrounding forest. It would be peaceful if not for the circumstances.

"How are you holding up?" Lennon asks, studying my face. "You look pale."

"I'm fine," I say automatically, then catch myself. This is Lennon. I don't have to pretend with her. "Actually, I'm terrified.

What if they don't let him out? What if Noah finds some way to keep him locked up?"

"That's not going to happen," Lennon assures me firmly. "Shawn's one of the best attorneys in the state, and Judge Holloway isn't in Morrison's pocket. The system doesn't always work, but today, it's working in our favor. She already told them to release the guys. It just takes a while for the wheels of justice to turn."

I want to believe her. I need to believe her. "And the rustling charges? What if they stick?"

She shakes her head. "Like I said, the evidence is circumstantial at best. They've got some grainy video footage and Morrison's word, which isn't worth much once people find out what he's been planning with Project Watershed."

"What exactly is Project Watershed?" I ask. It's been mentioned before, but no one has really explained it to me.

"It's a land grab," Lennon says, her expression hardening. "The Morrisons are trying to buy up all the land around the river and its tributaries. Once they control the water rights, they can charge whatever they want for access. They'd essentially control who gets to ranch in Grizzly River."

"And that's legal?"

"It's in a gray area," she admits. "But that's not the point. The point is, once the other ranchers understand what's at stake, they'll see Devlin and the others as the ones fighting back against corporate greed, not as criminals."

Before I can respond, the jail doors swing open, and my heart leaps into my throat. Jesse emerges first, followed by Truett and Carson. Then there he is, Devlin, his broad shoulders filling out a plain white T-shirt that's clearly not his own. Even from here, I can see the angry red mark on his face where Noah struck him. It looks like they gave him clothes because he may have gotten blood on his.

I don't think, don't hesitate. I'm running before I realize I've pushed off from the SUV, my feet carrying me across the parking lot, dodging a patrol car that's pulling in.

"Devlin!" I call out, and his head snaps up, his eyes finding mine.

Something in his face changes when he sees me, the hard lines softening, the tension in his jaw easing. He takes a few steps forward, opening his arms just as I launch myself at him.

His arms close around me, solid and warm and real, lifting me slightly off the ground as I bury my face in his neck, breathing in his scent. He smells like cheap soap and something distinctly him beneath it, and I've never been so grateful for anything in my life.

"You're okay," I whisper against his skin, my voice choked with emotion. "You're really okay."

"I'm okay," he confirms, his lips brushing my temple. "Everything's going to be fine, Atlee. I promise."

I pull back just enough to examine his face, my fingers ghosting over the split in his lip and the bruise forming on his cheekbone. "He hurt you."

A small, dangerous smile curves his mouth. "Trust me, it was worth it. Played right into our hands."

I want to argue that nothing is worth his being hurt, but this isn't the time or place. "Let's go home," I say instead. "I want to get you away from here."

He nods, keeping one arm around me as we walk toward my SUV. Jesse calls out something about meeting tomorrow, and

Devlin raises a hand in acknowledgment, but his focus remains on me.

Once we're in the car, doors closed against the outside world, he turns to me, his expression serious. "I'm sorry you had to find out this way. We had a plan, but things moved faster than we expected."

"Lennon filled me in on some of it," I tell him, starting the engine. "She seems to think it's all going to work out."

"It will," he says with quiet confidence. "Noah overplayed his hand, and the Morrisons are about to have bigger problems than us tomorrow."

I navigate out of the parking lot, heading toward home—our home, I remind myself with a small thrill despite the circumstances. It still feels strange to think of Devlin's cabin as mine too, but in the best possible way.

"What happened exactly?" I ask as we drive, needing to understand all of it.

He tells me about Austin's warning, about Noah and the deputies bursting into the barn, about the arrest, and about Noah's unnecessary violence. His voice remains steady, but I can see the tension in the set of his shoulders and hear the controlled anger when he describes Noah striking him.

"He wanted me to fight back," Devlin explains. "Give him an excuse to escalate. But that's not how this game is played."

"This isn't a game," I say, gripping the steering wheel tighter. "This is your life, Devlin. Your freedom."

He reaches over, placing his hand on my thigh, the warmth of it seeping through my jeans. "I know that. But trust me, we've got this under control. This isn't the first tight spot I've been in, and it won't be the last."

Something about his calm certainty steadies me. This is the man who survived multiple combat tours, who built a life for himself from nothing when he returned. If anyone can navigate this storm, it's him.

The rest of the drive passes in comfortable silence, his hand remaining on my leg. It's exactly what I need to ground me and remind me he's actually here with me.

When we pull up to the cabin, the sight of it fills me with relief—the solid wooden walls, the porch where we've spent so many evenings, the rocking chairs side by side facing the mountains.

"It's good to be home," Devlin says softly, as if reading my thoughts.

Inside, the half-finished shelving units still sit in the living room, a reminder of the life we were planning before everything went sideways. Devlin stands in the middle of the room, looking around as if seeing it for the first time, or maybe just appreciating it in a new way after his brief confinement.

"You should clean up," I tell him, gesturing to his face. "Let me get you some ice for that bruise."

He catches my wrist as I turn toward the kitchen, pulling me back against his chest. "In a minute," he murmurs, his breath warm against my ear. "Right now, I just want to hold you."

I melt into him, letting his strength envelop me. His hands slide up my back, into my hair, tilting my face up to his. The kiss is gentle, mindful of his injured lip, but there's an intensity behind it that steals my breath.

"I was so scared," I confess when we break apart. "When Lennon called and said you'd been arrested..."

"I know," he says, his forehead resting against mine. "But I'm here now, and nothing—not Noah, not the Morrisons, nothing—is going to take me away from you. I promise."

There's a fierce certainty in his voice that makes me believe him, despite all evidence to the contrary, despite the charges hanging over his head, and despite the powerful men aligned against him.

His hands frame my face, thumbs stroking over my cheekbones. "You believe me, don't you?"

"Yes," I whisper, and I mean it. "I believe you."

His expression shifts, a hunger replacing the tenderness. His next kiss is deeper, more urgent, his hands dropping to my hips to pull me firmly against him. I respond instantly, my body recognizing what we both need right now, to connect with one another and make sure both of us are okay.

My fingers find the hem of his shirt, slipping underneath to touch warm skin. He makes a sound low in his throat, half growl, half groan, and suddenly we're moving, stumbling toward the bedroom, shedding clothes as we go.

When we tumble onto the bed, the familiarity surrounds me —the laundry detergent I picked out last week, the subtle musk that's uniquely Devlin. It smells like home, like safety, and everything I've always wanted.

His body covers mine, solid and warm, his weight the most welcome pressure I've ever felt. I run my hands over every inch of him I can reach, reassuring myself that he's here, he's whole, he's mine. My lips run up and down his flesh, wanting to imprint myself on every part of him.

"I love you," I whisper against his skin, as he presses his length deep into my body. "I love you so much."

"Atlee," he breathes my name as he presses in and pulls out of me. "My Atlee."

There's a desperation in our lovemaking that's never been there before. The reality of knowing it could be pulled away from us as quickly as we got it has me pressing my head back against the pillow and glancing up at Devlin. His face is a mask of passion as he presses his knees against the mattress and completely decimates my body.

He's a man on a mission as he reaches down between us and presses his thumb to my clit, causing me to fall apart in his arms. As my body grips his, he throws his head back and grunts as I feel his release. Panting, I try to slow down my pounding heart.

After, as we lie tangled in the sheets, his heartbeat steady beneath my ear, I trace the tattoos on his chest, following the intricate patterns that tell the story of his life before me.

"Do you think it will always be like this?" I ask quietly. "People trying to come between us?"

He's silent for a moment, his fingers drawing lazy circles on my bare shoulder. "Not always," he finally says. "Noah and the Morrisons...they're just obstacles. We'll get past them."

"And then?"

"And then we build a life," he says simply. "The one we were planning before all this happened. The shelves, the porch swing, maybe a garden in the spring."

I smile against his skin, loving the picture he's painting. "That sounds perfect."

"It will be," he promises, pressing a kiss to the top of my head. "I'm not letting anything take that future away from us, Atlee. Nothing and no one."

I believe him. Despite everything—the charges, Noah's

vendetta, the uncertainty of what tomorrow will bring—I believe him. Because if there's one thing I've learned about Devlin Nelson, it's that when he sets his mind to something, not even the forces of nature can stand in his way.

And right now, his mind is set on us. On our future together. On the life we're building in this small cabin on the edge of the Grizzly River Ranch.

As I drift toward sleep, secure in the circle of his arms, I look forward to the rest of my life with him. Whatever comes next, we'll face it together. And somehow, I know that will be enough.

TWENTY-TWO
DEVLIN

I WAKE UP WITH A START. For a moment, I'm disoriented, the memory of jail cells and plastic restraints too fresh in my mind. Then I feel Atlee's warm body curled against mine, her breathing deep and even in sleep, and reality settles back into place.

I'm home. We're safe. For now.

I lie there watching as the first light of morning filters through the curtains, casting soft shadows across Atlee's sleeping face. She soothes the restlessness in me and quiets the constant noise in my head. Even now, with charges hanging over my head and Noah gunning for me, I find a measure of peace just watching her sleep.

But the peace doesn't last. As the room grows lighter, my thoughts turn to the day ahead. The article about Project Watershed should be hitting the website and the regular paper today, exposing Morrison's plan to control the water rights throughout the county. It's a good plan, one that should shift public opinion in our favor, but it also makes us bigger targets for Noah and the Morrisons—if they dare to not let this go. I'm hoping they do, but we don't know until we see what others in the county think about this.

That means Atlee could be an even bigger target too.

She stirs beside me, her eyes fluttering open, immediately finding mine as if she sensed I was watching her. A sleepy smile curves her lips.

"Morning," she murmurs, her voice husky with sleep.

"Morning," I reply, brushing a strand of dark hair from her face. "Sleep okay?"

She nods, stretching like a cat, all curves and claws. "Better than I expected, considering."

I know what she means. Yesterday was a hell of a day, the kind that should have kept us both tossing and turning. But there's something about being together that makes even the worst days bearable.

"What time do you have to be at work?" I ask, already formulating a plan for the day.

"Nine," she says, glancing at the clock on the bedside table. "Why?"

I sit up, the sheet pooling around my waist. "I don't want you driving yourself today. Not with everything that's going on."

A small frown creases her forehead. "Devlin..."

"It's not just being overprotective," I cut in, though we both know that's part of it. "I don't trust Noah. He's desperate, and desperate men do stupid things."

The frown deepens. "You think he'd come after me?"

"I think he'd do anything to get to me right now," I say

honestly. "Including using you. I'd just feel better if I took you to work and picked you up after."

She studies my face for a long moment, and I can see her weighing her independence against my concern. Finally, she nods. "Okay. But I'm not going to live in fear, Devlin. We can't let Noah and the Morrisons dictate how we live our lives."

"We won't," I promise, leaning down to press a kiss to her forehead. "This is just until things settle down. Once the dust clears from the article dropping, we'll reassess."

She seems satisfied with that, or at least willing to humor me for now. We get ready together, moving around each other with the easy familiarity of a couple who've been together far longer than we have. It's still new enough to make my chest tighten with something like wonder, this simple domestic routine—brushing teeth side by side at the sink, sharing the mirror, her reaching around me for her hairbrush, me stealing a kiss as we pass in the hallway.

After a quick breakfast, we head out to my truck. The morning is crisp, frost glittering on the grass and the promise of winter in the air. Atlee shivers slightly, pulling her jacket tighter around herself.

"Getting cold," she comments as we climb into the truck. "Snow won't be far behind."

"Couple of weeks, probably," I agree, starting the engine.

The drive into town is quiet, both of us lost in our own thoughts. I take the back roads, avoiding the main highway where we might run into Noah or his deputies. It's longer this way, but safer, and the scenery is better, with dense pine forests giving way to open meadows and the mountains rising majestically in the distance.

As we near town, I can feel myself tensing, eyes constantly checking the mirrors, scanning for patrol cars. Atlee notices, her hand finding mine on the gearshift.

"It's going to be okay," she says softly. "Lennon seems confident the charges won't stick."

"Yeah," I say, though I'm less confident than I let on. Not about the charges—those are flimsy at best—but about what Noah might do in retaliation once the article drops. Men like him, they don't take public humiliation well.

I pull up in front of Murphy's General Store, parking right by the entrance where the morning crowd can see us clearly. Let them look. Let them talk. I want everyone in Grizzly River to know I'm not hiding. I'm not running from the accusations against me.

"Text me when your shift is over," I tell Atlee, leaning across the center console to kiss her goodbye. "I'll be here to pick you up."

"I will," she promises, her fingers lingering on my cheek. "Be careful today. Don't do anything reckless."

I smile despite myself. "Me? Reckless?"

She rolls her eyes, but she's smiling too. "You know what I mean. Stay out of trouble."

"Yes, ma'am," I drawl, giving her a mock salute.

She shakes her head, still smiling as she climbs out of the truck. I wait until she's safely inside the store before pulling away, heading toward my next destination, the Grizzly River Feed & Supply.

We need to restock some items at the ranch, and, more importantly, I need to get a sense of how the town is reacting to the article. The feed store is the unofficial hub of Grizzly River's gossip network. If people are talking about Project Watershed, this is where I'll hear it.

I park out front, noting that the lot is unusually full for this time of morning. Interesting. Inside, the store is buzzing with activity, with ranchers and townspeople clustered in small groups, all of them talking animatedly. The conversation dies down as I walk in, and I brace myself for dirty looks and whispered accusations.

Instead, a slow clap starts from somewhere in the back of the store. It spreads, person by person, until nearly everyone is applauding. I stop in my tracks, looking around in confusion, not sure what the hell is happening.

Phillip Reeves, the store's owner, steps forward, a copy of the *Grizzly River Gazette* clutched in his weathered hand. "About damn time somebody stood up to the Morrisons," he says, clapping me on the shoulder. "We all appreciate what you Nelson boys and Truett Weber have done."

I blink, caught off guard by the unexpected support. "I'm not sure what you're talking about," I say, playing dumb even as relief washes through me. The article worked. It actually worked.

Phillip gives me a knowing look, holding up the newspaper. "This exposé on Project Watershed," he says. "How the Morrisons have been buying up water rights all across the county, planning to choke out the smaller ranches."

I take the paper, scanning the front-page article. It's even more damning than I expected, naming both the Morrisons and Noah. I didn't know they'd be mentioning Noah too.

"Where'd this information come from?" I ask, handing the paper back.

"Anonymous sources," Phillip says with a wink. "But word is, you boys had something to do with bringing it to light and then got arrested for your trouble."

"Wouldn't know anything about that." I shrug.

Another rancher, Bill Thompson, joins us. "Doesn't take a genius to figure out what happened," he says gruffly. "They're in with the most crooked deputy we've ever had."

Part of me is slightly ashamed since we didn't start out doing this out of the goodness of our hearts, but if it's going to keep us out of hot water, then it is what it is. Hopefully, by the time we're done, we'll be able to pay back anyone we harmed.

"Noah Sanchez is a disgrace to the badge," someone else chimes in. "Always has been. Even back in high school, he was dangerous."

The conversation flows around me, everyone eager to share their opinions of Noah, the Morrisons, and the cattle rustling charges against us. It's clear which side they're on.

"Well," I say finally. "I appreciate the support. But we've still got legal issues to sort out."

"You'll beat those charges," Phillip assures me. "Nobody's going to convict you boys for standing up to the Morrisons. Not in this county."

"From your lips to God's ears," I murmur.

I place my order for feed and supplies, and Phillip insists on giving me a discount. "For all the trouble," he explains with a shrug.

As I wait for my order to be filled, more people approach to express their support. Some I know well, others just by sight, a few not at all.

By the time I leave, loaded down with supplies and a

newfound sense of cautious optimism, it's mid-morning. I head back to my truck, scanning the street for any sign of Noah or his deputies. The coast seems clear, but I remain vigilant as I load the supplies.

Just as I'm about to climb into the driver's seat, a familiar voice calls my name. I turn to see Austin jogging toward me, a copy of the Gazette in his hand.

"Have you seen this?" he asks, slightly out of breath. "It's all over town."

"Just read it," I confirm. "Phillip and the others in the feed store are pretty worked up about it."

Austin grins, looking pleased. "It's working, Devlin. The whole plan is actually working."

I glance around, making sure no one's within earshot. "Let's not celebrate yet. Noah and the Morrisons won't take this lying down."

His smile fades slightly. "Yeah, I know. But for the first time, I feel like we might actually win this thing."

"Maybe." I allow, not wanting to dampen his enthusiasm completely. "How are Jesse and Truett taking all this?"

"Jesse is in a meeting with Shawn Cooper, going over legal strategy," Austin says. "Truett is back at the ranch, keeping an eye on things there. We figured it was best not to all be in town at once. Makes it harder for Noah to track us."

I nod, approving of their caution. "Smart. Any sign of Noah or his deputies today?"

Austin shakes his head. "Nothing so far. Word is, he's holed up at the station, not taking calls. The sheriff is supposedly on the warpath about the article, demanding to know why he wasn't briefed about Project Watershed."

"Good," I say grimly. "Let them fight among themselves for a while. Takes the heat off us."

"Speaking of heat," Austin says, lowering his voice. "Have you heard from Carson? He was supposed to check in this morning, but no one's been able to reach him."

A thread of unease winds through me. Carson is the one who put himself on the line by hacking and gathering all the intel we needed. If he's gone silent...

"I'll try him," I say, pulling out my phone. "He might just be lying low after the article dropped."

Austin nods, but I can see he's worried too. "Let me know if you hear from him. Jesse is getting antsy."

"Will do," I promise, clapping him on the shoulder. "In the meantime, keep your head down. This isn't over yet."

He gives me a mock salute, similar to the one I gave Atlee earlier, before jogging back down the street toward his own truck.

I climb into my vehicle and immediately try Carson's number. It rings several times before going to voicemail. I hang up without leaving a message—better not to create a record if he's in a sensitive situation—and instead send a text that looks innocuous to anyone who might be monitoring his phone.

Me
Mom's asking about Sunday dinner.
You in?

It's our code for checking in. If he responds with anything about bringing dessert, it means he's fine but can't talk. If he mentions a side dish, it means he's in trouble.

No response comes as I pull away from the feed store,

heading back toward the ranch. The optimism I felt earlier is tempered now by concern for Carson. He's the youngest of us brothers, always trying to prove himself. I hope his eagerness hasn't gotten him into a situation he can't handle.

The road back to the ranch is clear, with no sign of patrol cars or suspicious vehicles. Still, I take a circuitous route, doubling back a couple of times to ensure I'm not being followed. Old habits from my military days, but they've kept me alive this long.

As I drive, my thoughts return to Atlee. I should have warned her this morning about the article and prepared her for the attention it might bring. She's smart, adaptable. She'll handle it fine, but I still don't like the idea of her being caught off guard.

I send her a quick text at a stoplight.

Me
The town is talking about the Morrisons and Project Watershed. Article in the Gazette. Might get questions. Call if you need me.

Her response comes almost immediately.

Atlee
Already fielded three "casual" inquiries. Don't worry. Playing dumb like a pro. Be safe.

I can't help but smile at that. She's tougher than most give her credit for, my Atlee.

By the time I reach the turnoff to the ranch, my phone is buzzing with texts from Jesse, Truett, and even Lennon, all of them reacting to the article and the town's response. The general consensus seems to be positive. The tide of public opinion is turning in our favor, exactly as we'd hoped.

But Carson still hasn't responded, and that worry gnaws at me as I drive the final stretch to the ranch. If the Morrisons have figured out that he's been feeding us information...I don't want to think about what they might do. Richard Morrison didn't get to where he is by playing nice.

As I pull up to the ranch house, I see Truett waiting on the porch, pacing back and forth with barely contained energy. He bounds down the steps as I park, eager for news.

"Town's buzzing," I tell him before he can ask. "Everyone has read the article. They're on our side."

Relief floods his face. "Thank God. We needed a win."

"It's just the first round," I caution, climbing out of the truck. "Morrison and Noah won't take this lying down."

"Let 'em come," Truett says with the bravado of youth. "The whole county is against them now."

I wish I shared his confidence, but I've seen too much, been through too many battles to believe any victory is assured until it's over. Still, it's good to see hope in his eyes again after weeks of strain and worry.

"Heard from Carson?" I ask, changing the subject.

Truett's expression darkens. "Not a word. Jesse's about ready to tear the county apart looking for him."

"Let's not panic yet," I say, though my own concern is growing by the minute. "Carson is smart. He knows how to handle himself."

"Yeah," Truett agrees, but he doesn't sound convinced. "Jesse wants to meet when you get back. Plan our next move."

I nod and unload the supplies from the truck bed. "I'll be

there. Just need to check in with Atlee first and make sure she's okay."

"She at work?" Truett asks, helping me with a particularly heavy bag of feed.

"Yeah, at the pharmacy. I'm picking her up when her shift ends."

He gives me a knowing look. "Still worried about Noah coming after her?"

"Wouldn't you be?" I counter.

He concedes the point with a shrug. "Fair enough. But after this article, Noah's going to have his hands full. Might not have time for revenge plots."

"Maybe," I allow, but I'm not taking chances. Not with Atlee's safety.

As we carry the supplies into the barn, I'm struck by how quickly everything has changed. Just twenty-four hours ago, I was being arrested, facing serious charges, and uncertain of the future. Now, the town is rallying behind us, the Morrisons' scheme is exposed, and for the first time in months, it feels like we might actually come out on top.

But I know better than to count victories before they're won. There are still too many variables, too many ways this could all go sideways.

And Atlee, caught in the middle of it all because she chose me.

I check my phone again, hoping for a message from Carson, but there's nothing. Just a text from Atlee.

> **Atlee**
> Miss you. See you at 5.

Those simple words steady me and remind me what I'm fighting for. Not just the ranch, not just clearing our names, but a future with her. A life together that's not shadowed by threats and fear.

For that, I'd take on Noah, the Morrisons, and anyone else who stands in our way. Judging by the reaction in town today, we might not have to face them alone after all.

TWENTY-THREE
ATLEE

THE PHARMACY IS UNUSUALLY busy today. It seems like everybody who lives in Grizzly River has suddenly developed a need for cold medicine, vitamins, or prescription refills. But I'm not naïve enough to think it's coincidental, not with the way they're all looking at me, offering small smiles or nods of acknowledgment that go beyond the usual small-town friendliness.

Mrs. Henderson, who is picking up her blood pressure medication, lingers at the counter after I hand her the white paper bag.

"Your young man," she says, her voice lowered conspiratorially. "He's got real courage, that one."

I blink, caught off guard. "I'm sorry?"

"Devlin," she clarifies, as if I might be confused about which "young man" she means. "Standing up to the Morrisons like that. My Harold always said someone needed to put Richard in his place, but nobody had the guts. Until now."

"Oh," I say, unsure how to respond. "Well, thank you."

She pats my hand, her arthritic fingers surprisingly strong. "You hold on to him, dear. Men like that don't come along every day."

As she shuffles away, I catch Payton watching me from where she's restocking the shelves, a knowing smirk on her face.

"What was that about?" I ask once Mrs. Henderson is out of earshot.

Payton abandons her task, coming over to lean against the counter. "You really don't know? It's all anyone in town is talking about."

My stomach tightens. "The arrests?" Or is the article that I have to pretend like I know nothing about?

"No. Well...yes, that too, but mostly the article." She reaches behind the counter, producing a copy of the *Grizzly River Gazette* that I hadn't noticed before. "Front page."

I take the paper, my eyes immediately drawn to the bold headline.

"Morrison Land Grab Threatens County Water Rights."

Beneath it is a detailed exposé about Project Watershed, how Richard Morrison and his family have been systematically buying up land around the county's water sources, and positioning themselves to control who gets water access and at what price.

The article quotes anonymous sources close to the investigation, detailing not just the land purchases but also backroom deals with county officials, including Deputy Noah Sanchez, who reportedly helped pressure reluctant landowners to sell.

"Oh my god, it actually came out," I breathe in a whisper,

scanning through the damning accusations. No wonder the town is buzzing.

"Yeah," Payton says, a hint of admiration in her voice. "And word is, your boyfriend and his brothers are the ones who exposed it all. Got arrested for their trouble too."

"That's why everyone's been looking at me like that," I realize, thinking back on the parade of customers who've passed through today, each with a knowing look or encouraging word.

"You're dating a local hero," Payton confirms. "How does it feel?"

I'm not sure how to answer that. Pride swells in my chest at the thought of Devlin standing up to the Morrisons, risking everything to protect the other ranchers. But fear coils alongside it. This is all out in the open now.

"It feels..." I search for the right word. "Complicated."

Payton laughs. "I bet. Well, brace yourself, because you've got another admirer incoming."

I look up to see Mr. Daniels, who owns the hardware store down the street, approaching the counter with a prescription slip in hand.

"Atlee," he greets me, his weathered face creasing into a smile. "How's that man of yours holding up after yesterday? Damned travesty, those arrests."

And so it goes for the rest of the morning. By lunchtime, I've stopped being surprised by it and started accepting their well-wishes with simple gratitude.

"You tell Devlin that we're behind him all the way," Ellie Travers says as she picks up her son's asthma medication. "My husband is already talking about organizing the other ranchers. We're not letting the Morrisons get away with this water grab."

"I'll tell him," I promise, touched by how quickly the town has rallied.

When there's finally a lull in customers, I text Devlin again after he checked on me earlier.

Me
Everyone at the pharmacy has read the article. You've got a lot of supporters in town. Even Mrs. Henderson called you courageous, and she doesn't impress easily.

Devlin
Glad to hear it. Stay alert, though. Noah won't take this lying down.

The warning sends a chill through me, but I push aside the fear. I refuse to let Noah Sanchez dictate how I live my life.

"You must be very proud," Reverend Miller says as I ring up his allergy medication.

And I realize with a start that I am. Fiercely, unequivocally proud to be with a man who stands up for what's right, even when it's dangerous. Even when it comes at a personal cost.

"Yes," I tell the reverend, a smile spreading across my face. "I am."

He nods approvingly. "Good. He'll need that pride and belief in the days ahead. The Morrisons won't surrender easily."

The reminder of the battle still to come sobers me, but doesn't diminish the warmth in my chest. Whatever happens next, Devlin won't face it alone. He has me, he has his brothers, and now, it seems, he has most of Grizzly River standing behind him too.

As closing time approaches, I start the end-of-day routine.

Payton has already left, her shift ending an hour before mine. I'm alone in the pharmacy section, the store quiet around me as the last few shoppers finish their business in the grocery section.

I check my phone, seeing a message from Devlin.

Devlin
Running a bit late. Wait inside for me?

I text him back.

Me
Will do.

I get back to finishing closing procedures. The quiet is peaceful after the busy day, giving me time to process everything that's happened. In just a few weeks, my life has transformed completely. I went from someone who didn't know if they'd ever find love to finding it and being happy with it.

I'm so absorbed in my thoughts that I don't immediately register the bell above the door chiming, signaling someone's entrance. It's only when I hear the gasps and startled exclamations from the few remaining customers that I look up.

My blood freezes in my veins.

Noah Sanchez stands in the doorway, his uniform rumpled, his face flushed with what might be anger or alcohol or both. But it's not his disheveled appearance that stops my heart. It's the gun in his hand, pressed against Carson's temple.

"Everyone stay calm," Noah announces, his voice carrying through the suddenly silent store. "This is official police business."

Carson's eyes find mine, wide with fear but also a warning.

His hands are zip-tied in front of him, his lip bleeding from what looks like a recent blow.

"Noah," I say carefully, stepping out from behind the pharmacy counter. "What are you doing?"

His gaze snaps to me, and there's something unhinged in his eyes that terrifies me more than the gun. "Atlee Walsh," he says, almost conversationally. "Just the woman I was hoping to see."

He shoves Carson forward, keeping the gun trained on him as they move further into the store. The few customers have pressed themselves against the walls, trying to become invisible. All except one, a teenager who's holding up his cell phone, the telltale red recording light visible from where I stand.

"You," Noah barks, noticing the boy. "What are you doing?"

The teenager flinches but doesn't lower his phone. "L-live streaming," he stammers. "For my Insta."

Something shifts in Noah's expression, a calculated gleam replacing the wild look. "Perfect," he says, surprising us all. "Keep that camera rolling, kid. I want everyone to see this."

He turns back to me, gesturing with the gun. "Come here, Atlee. Nice and slow."

Every instinct screams at me to run, but I can't leave Carson. I move forward cautiously, hands raised to show I'm not a threat. "Noah, think about what you're doing. This isn't going to solve anything."

"Shut up," he snaps, grabbing my arm when I get close enough. He pulls me roughly against his side, the gun now alternating between pointing at Carson and me. "Both of you, over by the window where everyone can see us."

We comply, moving to the large front window that faces the main street. Through the glass, I can see people stopping on the sidewalk, pointing, some already on their phones, calling the police, I hope. Though what good that will do when the threat is a deputy himself, I don't know.

"Noah," Carson tries, his voice admirably steady despite the circumstances. "You're making this worse for yourself."

"Worse?" Noah laughs, the sound brittle and harsh. "How could it get worse? I'm already finished in this town after that article. Suspended pending investigation." He spits the words like they taste foul. "Twenty years on the force, and they suspend me on the word of a bunch of cattle thieves."

His grip on my arm tightens painfully, and I wince. "You can still walk away from this," I tell him. "No one's been hurt yet. You could—"

"I said shut up," he cuts me off, jerking me closer. To the boy with the phone, he says, "Make sure you're getting all this, kid. I want Devlin Nelson to see exactly what's happening here."

My heart sinks. This is about Devlin. Of course it is.

"Hey, Nelson!" Noah shouts, clearly playing to the camera now. "You seeing this? Your girlfriend and your brother, right here with me. How does it feel knowing I can take everything from you, just like you took everything from me?"

The desperation in his voice is palpable, the bitterness of a man who feels he has nothing left to lose. Those are the most dangerous people—the ones with no exit strategy, no reason to de-escalate.

"If you're watching this," Noah continues, addressing the phone. "You have thirty minutes to get here. You and everyone else who's plotted against me, or things are going to get very unpleasant for these two." He nudges the gun against my ribs for emphasis. "Clock's ticking, fucker."

The boy with the phone looks terrified but keeps recording, the red light a steady beacon in the chaos.

"Please," I say quietly, trying one more time to reach whatever rationality might be left in Noah. "You don't have to do this. Whatever happened between you and Devlin is in the past."

"You don't know anything about it," Noah hisses, his face inches from mine. "About what he took from me."

"Then tell me," I urge, hoping to keep him talking, to humanize myself in his eyes. "Help me understand."

For a moment, I think he might actually explain, might give me some insight into the hatred that's driven him to this desperate act. But then his expression hardens again.

"Nice try," he says coldly. "But I'm not falling for your psychological tricks. You just stand there and look pretty for the camera. Your boyfriend will be here soon enough."

My stomach twists at the thought of Devlin walking into this trap. He will come. I know he will as surely as I know my own name. Nothing could keep him away, knowing I'm in danger, and his brothers will be right beside him.

Which is exactly what Noah is counting on.

"What's your endgame here, Noah?" Carson asks, voice low. "You think you can take on all the Nelsons? Even if you manage it, the whole town will be after you."

Noah's laugh is hollow. "You think I care about that anymore? I've got nothing left. My career is over. My reputation is ruined. Might as well go out making sure Devlin Nelson pays for what he did."

The single-minded focus of his vendetta would be almost admirable if it weren't so terrifying. This isn't about justice or even the law anymore. This is personal—the kind of hatred that consumes everything in its path.

I glance at the boy with the phone, wondering if the livestream has reached Devlin yet and if he's watching this unfold in real-time. I hope not. I hope he's busy, his phone forgotten in his truck while he works. I hope he doesn't see me like this, held at gunpoint because of my connection to him.

But even as I think it, I know it's a futile hope. Devlin will come, and when he does, Noah will be waiting, gun in hand and revenge in his heart.

All I can do is stay calm, stay alert, and look for any opportunity to change the outcome of this confrontation. Because I refuse to be the reason Devlin walks into a bullet. I refuse to be Noah's instrument of revenge.

Outside, the street has cleared, people taking cover in nearby stores or behind parked cars. Someone must have called in the situation because I can hear sirens in the distance. But will they arrive in time? And who will respond if not Noah and his deputies?

"Hear that?" I say, nodding toward the sound. "That's backup coming. The sheriff, probably. You still have time to end this peacefully."

Noah's grip tightens again, the barrel of the gun pressing painfully into my side. "Shut. Up."

I fall silent, catching Carson's eye across the small space between us. There's a silent communication there, a promise that we'll get through this, that we'll find a way out. I hold on to that promise as the minutes tick by, as the sirens draw closer, and as we wait for whatever comes next.

Because one thing is certain. Devlin is coming, and when he arrives, everything will change.

TWENTY-FOUR
DEVLIN

THE CALL COMES as I'm heading to pick up Atlee from work. Jesse's voice on the phone is tight, controlled, and trying not to let panic take over.

"Noah's got Carson and Atlee at the pharmacy. He's armed."

Everything inside me goes cold, a familiar stillness settling over me like a second skin. It's the same feeling I had in combat, with time slowing down, senses sharpening, all emotion receding behind a wall that I had to keep closed off to everything.

"How do you know?" I ask, pressing the gas pedal down harder.

"Some kid was livestreaming it. Noah's calling you out. He wants you and the rest of us to show up. He looks unhinged, Devlin. He's got a gun on both of them."

I press harder, the engine roaring in protest. "Where are you now?"

"About ten minutes out. Truett's with me."

"Don't come in guns blazing," I instruct, falling back into the role of commander without thinking. "Noah is unstable. He sees all of us charging in, he might do something stupid."

"What are you thinking?"

"I go in alone," I say, the decision already made. "Talk him down if I can."

"And if you can't?" he questions, voice terrified.

I don't answer that. We both know what happens if I can't talk him down.

"I'll be there in five," I tell Jesse instead. "Call the sheriff. Make sure he knows it's one of his deputies in there."

I end the call before he can argue, focusing on the road ahead. My mind is already running through scenarios, tactics, and contingency plans. The skills I honed in special ops come back like muscle memory.

By the time I reach town, the main street has been cordoned off. Sheriff's deputies, the ones not loyal to Noah, have established a perimeter around Murphy's General Store. An ambulance idles nearby, paramedics standing ready. A small crowd has gathered behind the barricades, faces tense with concern.

I spot Sheriff Taylor himself coordinating the response, his weathered face grim as he speaks into a radio. When he sees me, he waves me over.

"Nelson," he greets me tersely. "Figured you'd show up."

"What's the situation?" I ask, scanning the storefront. From this angle, I can't see inside the pharmacy section, but I know the layout by heart.

"Sanchez has your girl and Carson hostage in the pharmacy. He's made it clear he wants you and the rest of your brothers to come in. Says he'll shoot them both if you don't show."

"I'm going in," I state, not a question.

Taylor studies me, weighing his options. "You have military training, right? Special ops?"

I nod.

"Thought so." He gestures to one of his deputies. "Get Mr. Nelson a vest."

The deputy hurries to comply, returning with a bulletproof vest. I shrug off my jacket and strap it on, knowing it won't stop everything but grateful for the protection nonetheless.

"Plan?" Taylor asks, all business now.

"I go in alone," I tell him. "Noah wants me? He gets me. But just me. My brothers stay out here. Less chance of someone getting trigger-happy that way."

"And once you're in?"

"I talk him down if I can. If not..." I let the implication hang. "Priority is getting Atlee and Carson out safely."

Taylor nods grimly. "We'll have snipers in position, but with the way that building is laid out, they don't have a clear shot inside the pharmacy area."

"I'll handle it," I assure him. "Just keep my brothers from charging in after me, no matter what they hear."

"Will do." He hands me a small earpiece. "Take this. It lets us communicate if needed."

I fit the device into my ear, testing it with a quick, "Check."

"We hear you," comes the reply from one of the deputies monitoring the comm system.

Jesse and Truett arrive as I'm doing a final check of my equipment. Their faces are masks of barely contained rage when they see me suited up.

"No," Jesse says immediately, reading my intention. "We go in together."

"Not this time," I counter, my tone leaving no room for argument. "He wants all of us in there to maximize his chances. I'm not giving him what he wants."

"Devlin—"

"He has Atlee," I cut him off, my voice dropping low. "I'm not risking her life by sending in a cavalry. This is how it has to be."

Something in my face must convince him, because he backs down, though reluctantly. "What's your play?"

"Get in, get them out," I say simply. "Noah's not thinking clearly. I can use that."

"And if he shoots you on sight?" Truett challenges.

"He won't," I say with more confidence than I feel. "He wants to gloat first. Wants me to know he won."

The sheriff approaches again, his radio crackling. "We've got a visual on Sanchez and the hostages. They're near the front window. Sanchez is agitated and keeps checking his watch."

"Time to move," I say, rolling my shoulders to loosen the tension. "Keep the perimeter secure, and no matter what happens in there, don't let anyone else in until I give the all clear. Understood?"

Taylor nods, then offers his hand. "Good luck, Nelson."

I shake it briefly, then turn to Jesse and Truett. "If this goes south, take care of Atlee for me."

Before they can respond, I'm moving toward the store entrance, hands raised to show I'm not holding a weapon, though I've got a Glock tucked in the back of my jeans, hidden beneath my shirt. Some habits die hard.

"I'm going in," I say into the earpiece. "Maintain radio silence unless absolutely necessary."

"Copy that," comes the terse reply.

The store is eerily quiet as I push through the front doors, the usual background music silenced. A few customers are huddled behind shelves, too frightened to make a run for the exit. I signal them to stay down, moving carefully toward the pharmacy section at the back.

Then I see them. Atlee and Carson are standing near the pharmacy window, Noah behind them with his service weapon drawn. His uniform is disheveled, eyes wild with a mixture of rage and something like fear or mania—the desperation of a man who's lost everything and has nothing left to lose.

But all I really see is Atlee. Her eyes find mine immediately, a complex mixture of relief and terror in her gaze. She looks unharmed, though her posture is rigid with tension.

"Devlin," Noah calls out, his voice echoing unnaturally loud in the silent store. "Finally decided to show up. Where are your brothers?"

"Just me," I reply, keeping my hands visible as I move closer. "Let them go, Noah. This is between us."

He laughs, the sound harsh and brittle. "Always the hero, aren't you? But I've got the upper hand this time."

"You do," I agree, stopping about ten feet away, close enough to talk but not close enough to rush him before he could get a shot off. "So let's talk."

"Talk?" he spits. "Like you talked to Jessalyn when you stole her away? Or like telling everybody about Project Watershed to get talk about the evidence ready to convict you out of the forefront of everyone's minds?"

I have to keep him talking. "What evidence?"

"Don't play dumb," Noah hisses, pressing the gun harder

against Atlee's side. She flinches, and it takes every ounce of self-control I have not to lunge forward. "I had proof of your cattle rustling. Tire tracks that matched your trucks, witness statements from one of Morrison's hands who saw the whole thing, camera footage. But now it's all circumstantial, and the grand jury refuses to indict? Coincidence? I don't think so."

I keep my expression neutral, though internally I'm happy since this is the first I'm hearing about the grand jury refusing to indict. That's really good news.

"I had nothing to do with that," I tell him. "But it doesn't matter now, does it? The whole town knows about Project Watershed. They're on our side."

"Your side?" Noah's voice rises, edged with hysteria. "You're criminals! Thieves! And they're treating you like heroes while I'm suspended pending investigation?"

"Noah," I say, keeping my voice calm, reasonable. "Think about what you're doing. Even if everything you believe about us is true, this isn't the way to handle it. You're holding innocent people at gunpoint."

"Innocent?" he scoffs. "Carson here is as guilty as the rest of you. And her?" He jerks Atlee closer. "She chose her side when she got involved with you."

I take a careful step forward, calculating distances, angles, and timing. "Let them go," I say again, my voice hardening. "Take me instead. I'm the one you really want."

For a moment, I think he's going to agree. His eyes flicker between his hostages and me, weighing options.

"Fine," he says finally. "Carson first. Then we'll talk about the girl."

He shoves Carson forward roughly. Carson stumbles but

catches himself, moving quickly toward me.

"Go," I tell him quietly as he reaches me. "Get out of here. Tell the sheriff what's happening."

He hesitates, clearly torn. "Devlin..."

"Go," I repeat, more firmly this time.

Carson nods once, then hurries toward the exit, leaving me alone with Noah and Atlee.

"Now let her go too," I say, turning my attention back to Noah.

He shakes his head, a cruel smile twisting his features. "Not a chance. She's my insurance policy."

I take another careful step forward. "This isn't going to end the way you want it to, Noah. The store is surrounded. You can't get out of here."

"Maybe I don't want to get out," he says, and there's something in his tone that chills me to the bone. "Maybe I just want to make sure you pay for what you did."

"And what exactly did I do?" I ask, playing for time, inching closer with each exchange. "Steal your high school girlfriend? That was fifteen years ago, Noah."

"It wasn't just Jessalyn," he snarls. "It was everything. The football scholarship I lost after you broke my ribs. The respect I worked for years to build in this town. And now my career."

"That wasn't me," I point out. "You did that to yourself when you got in bed with the Morrisons."

His face contorts with rage. "I know what you did! The cattle rustling, the break-ins at Morrison's office...all of it! I have proof!"

"No one will believe you," I tell him bluntly. "Not anymore.

Not after the article. The whole town sees us as the ones standing up against corruption. Against you and the Morrisons. Whatever evidence you think you have, it won't matter."

"Then I'll make them believe," he says, desperation bleeding into his voice. "One way or another."

I'm close enough now to see the sweat beading on his forehead, the slight tremor in the hand holding the gun. He's unraveling, and that makes him even more dangerous.

"Noah," I say, softening my tone. "It's over. Let Atlee go. We'll figure this out."

For a heartbeat, I think I've reached him. His eyes soften for just a moment.

Then his face hardens again. "No. If I'm going down, I'm taking you with me."

He swings the gun toward me, and I move on pure instinct. Diving to the side as the shot goes wide, I roll behind a display case, drawing my own weapon in one fluid motion.

"Atlee, down!" I shout, and thank God, she drops immediately, scrambling away from Noah.

Noah fires again, the bullet splintering the wood beside my head. I return fire, a controlled double tap aimed at his center mass. The first shot catches him in the shoulder, spinning him back. The second hits his leg, dropping him to the ground.

The gun falls from his hand, skittering across the floor. I'm on my feet instantly, kicking the weapon away before he can reach for it again.

Noah clutches his wounded shoulder, blood seeping between his fingers. His eyes burn with hatred as he looks up at me. "You won't get away with this," he gasps.

"It's already over," I tell him, keeping my gun trained on him as I back toward Atlee. "How are you doing, sweetheart? Are you hurt?"

"I'm okay," she says, her voice remarkably steady despite everything. "Carson?"

"Made it out," I assure her. "Are there any other customers still in the store?"

"A few," she says. "Hiding in the aisles."

I speak into my earpiece. "This is Devlin. Situation contained. Suspect is down but alive. Send in medical and clear the remaining civilians."

"Copy that," comes the immediate response. "Moving in now."

Noah is still conscious, still glaring at me with undiluted loathing. "This doesn't change anything," he slurs, the blood loss already affecting him. "They'll...find out what you did."

"Maybe," I acknowledge, holstering my weapon now that help is on the way. "But they'll also know what you did. Taking hostages, threatening innocent people. That's not something you come back from, Noah."

His eyes start to lose focus, his head lolling back against the floor. The fight's leaving him along with his blood, though the paramedics will be here soon enough to make sure he doesn't bleed out.

I turn to Atlee, pulling her into my arms at last. She's trembling slightly, the adrenaline crash hitting her, but her eyes are clear and determined.

"You came," she whispers against my chest.

"Of course I came," I murmur into her hair. "Nothing could have kept me away."

The store fills with deputies and paramedics, the hostage situation giving way to controlled chaos. Someone wraps a shock blanket around Atlee's shoulders, but she doesn't let go of me, her fingers twisted in the fabric of my shirt like she's afraid I'll disappear if she loosens her grip.

The paramedics work on Noah, stabilizing him for transport. His eyes are closed now, his face slack. He'll live to face charges —multiple counts of kidnapping, assault with a deadly weapon, and unlawful detention. His career isn't just over. His freedom is forfeit too.

Jesse and Truett burst in as soon as the all clear is given, their expressions a mixture of relief and residual anger.

"Everyone okay?" Jesse asks, his eyes taking in the scene—Noah on the stretcher, the bullet holes in the wall, Atlee still clinging to me.

"We're good," I tell him. "It's over."

But even as I say the words, I know it's not entirely true. Noah is neutralized, but the Morrisons are still out there, and they won't take the exposure of Project Watershed lying down. This is just one battle in a war that's far from over.

For now, though, all that matters is that Atlee is safe in my arms, Carson is unharmed, and my family is intact. We'll face whatever comes next together, just like we always have.

"Let's go home," I tell Atlee, pressing a kiss to her forehead.

She nods against my chest, finally relaxing her death grip on my shirt. "Home," she agrees, the word carrying all the weight of promise, of future, of the life we're building together despite everything trying to tear us apart.

As we walk out into the fading light of day, past the crowd and the flashing lights of emergency vehicles, I hold her close, my arm secure around her shoulders. Whatever happens next, whatever the Morrisons throw at us, this is what I'm fighting for —not just the ranch, not just my family's legacy, but the woman beside me who's become my reason for everything.

And God help anyone who tries to take her from me again.

TWENTY-FIVE
ATLEE

THE RIDE HOME from the pharmacy is quiet, both of us processing everything that happened. Devlin drives with one hand on the wheel, the other holding mine across the center console like he can't bear to break contact. I don't mind. After what we've been through today, I need that connection too—the solid warmth of his skin against mine, the gentle pressure of his fingers reminding me that we're both okay, we're both here.

The adrenaline has worn off, leaving me with a bone-deep exhaustion that makes even keeping my head up feel like a challenge. But beneath the fatigue, there's something else. There's a strange, fierce joy that we survived, that we're heading home together despite everything Noah tried to do.

"You okay?" Devlin asks, his voice low and gentle in the dimness of the truck cab. Sunset is painting the mountains in shades of gold and purple, casting long shadows across the road ahead.

"Yeah," I say, and I mean it. "Just tired. It's been a day."

He huffs a small laugh, the sound warm despite the understatement. "That it has."

We lapse back into silence as he turns down the long driveway to the cabin. The sight of it sends a wave of relief washing through me—the solid wooden walls, the porch with its rocking chairs, the glow of the automatic porch light welcoming us home. Home. It's amazing how quickly this place has become that to me.

Devlin parks, coming around to open my door before I can even unbuckle my seat belt. His protectiveness would have annoyed me once and made me feel smothered. Now I understand it's just his way of showing he cares.

"Come on," he says, helping me down from the truck, his hand lingering on the small of my back. "Let's get you inside."

But once we reach the porch, I hesitate. The evening is beautiful, crisp but not too cold. "Actually, can we sit out here for a bit? I could use some fresh air."

Devlin studies my face, then nods. "Whatever you need."

We settle into our rocking chairs, the wood creaking softly beneath us. The mountains rise before us, ancient and solid and unchanging, a reminder that today's drama is just a brief flash in the grand scheme of things.

"The article seems to have worked," Devlin says after a while, breaking the comfortable silence. "The town has rallied behind us. Morrison is going to have a hell of a time pushing Project Watershed through now that everyone knows what he's up to."

"Good," I say, feeling a fierce satisfaction at the thought of Richard Morrison's plans being thwarted. "He deserves to lose after what he tried to do."

Devlin makes a sound of agreement, his fingers tapping a restless rhythm against the armrest of his chair. There's something in his posture, a tension that tells me he has more on his mind than just Morrison's defeat.

"Noah won't be a problem anymore," he continues. "Even if he recovers, he's looking at serious jail time for what he did today."

"I know," I say, reaching across the space between our chairs to take his hand. "It's over, Devlin. We won."

He turns to look at me, his expression unreadable in the fading light. "Did we?"

"What do you mean?"

He sighs, running his free hand through his hair. "Just because Noah's out of the picture doesn't mean we're in the clear. The cattle rustling charges are still hanging over our heads, and Morrison isn't the type to give up easily."

"But the town is on your side now," I remind him. "And Shawn Cooper seems confident the charges won't stick."

"Maybe," he concedes. "But there's still a long road ahead."

I squeeze his hand. "And we'll face it together."

That gets a smile from him, small but genuine. "Together," he echoes, like he's testing the weight of the word.

We rock in silence for a few minutes, watching as the first stars begin to appear in the darkening sky. The peacefulness of the moment settles over us like a blanket, pushing back the remnants of fear and tension from the day's events.

"What would you say?" Devlin asks suddenly, his voice quiet but intent. "If I asked you to stay here forever?"

My heart stutters in my chest, and I turn to face him fully, searching his expression for what he's really asking. "Are you asking me to marry you?"

The directness of my question seems to catch him off guard. A flash of vulnerability crosses his face before he nods once, decisively. "Yes. I don't have a ring." He looks down at our linked hands, almost apologetic. "And this isn't how I planned to do it. But after today, after almost losing you, I don't want to wait for the perfect moment."

He shifts, turning his chair to face mine, both of his hands now holding mine. "I want you in my life forever, Atlee. I want to build something with you that lasts, something that's just ours. I know it's fast, and I know there's still a lot we're figuring out, but I've never been more certain of anything in my life."

Tears well up in my eyes, spilling over before I can stop them. Not sad tears, but the opposite. Tears of a joy so intense it almost hurts, of a certainty that matches his own.

"Yes," I whisper, the word catching on a half-laugh, half-sob. "Yes, I'll marry you."

The smile that breaks across his face is like a sunrise, slow at first, then brilliant, transforming his features with a joy that steals my breath. He pulls me from my chair onto his lap, his arms circling my waist, holding me like he never intends to let go.

"I love you," he says against my hair, his voice rough with emotion. "God, Atlee, I love you so much."

"I love you too," I whisper, framing his face with my hands, memorizing every line and plane of it in this moment. "More than I ever thought possible."

When he kisses me, it tastes of salt and promises. His lips are gentle at first, reverent, but the kiss quickly deepens into something more urgent, more needful. The day's fear and adrenaline transmute into desire, into a desperate need to reaffirm that we're alive, we're together, we're whole.

"We should go inside," I murmur against his mouth when we finally break apart, both of us breathing hard.

"In a minute," he says, pulling me closer against his chest, his heartbeat strong and steady beneath my ear. "Let's just stay here for a bit longer."

So we do, wrapped in each other's arms as night falls fully around us, the mountains fading into silhouettes against the star-studded sky. Despite everything—the danger we've faced and the challenges still ahead—I feel a peace I've never known before.

Because no matter what comes next, we'll face it together. Not just as Devlin and Atlee, but as husband and wife. Building a life, a future, a home that's ours alone.

Forever sounds just about right.

LENNON
EPILOGUE

I CHECK my watch for the third time in as many minutes, mentally calculating how late I'll be for dinner at this rate. Atlee is going to kill me. She's been planning this dinner with Aubree for weeks, some kind of celebration for their upcoming joint wedding shower. Being maid of honor for my sister and bridesmaid for her soon-to-be sister-in-law means twice the responsibility, and I'm already failing spectacularly.

The email from Shawn had come just as I was packing up to leave the office. "Just need your eyes on this before you go," he'd said, and of course, "this" turned out to be a sixty-page brief that needed immediate revisions. By the time I finished, the sun was already setting behind the mountains, casting long shadows across the winding road to Grizzly River Ranch.

I'm so focused on my lateness that I almost miss the concerning thump coming from the front passenger tire. By the time I register what's happening, the car is already pulling sharply to the right, the unmistakable flap-flap-flap of a flat tire forcing me to ease onto the shoulder.

"Perfect," I mutter, putting the car in park and dropping my head against the steering wheel. "Just perfect."

For a moment, I consider calling Atlee, but I can already picture her stressed expression as she tries to manage dinner preparations while sending someone to rescue me. No, better to handle this myself.

I grab my phone and step out of the car, shivering slightly in the early evening chill. Spring hasn't fully committed to Grizzly River yet. The days are warm, but the evenings still carry the coldness of winter. The light is fading fast, turning the deserted stretch of road into something from a horror movie—lonely woman, isolated location, no cell service.

Wait. No cell service?

I stare at my phone in disbelief. One bar, flickering in and out like it's taunting me. Of course.

Gritting my teeth, I pop the trunk and rummage around for the jack and spare tire. I've changed a flat before, once, in broad daylight, with my dad standing over my shoulder, barking instructions. How hard could it be to replicate that experience in near-darkness, alone, on a deserted road?

I'm struggling with the lug wrench, cursing under my breath, when headlights appear in the distance. For a split second, fear spikes through me. Then the lights slow, and a familiar pickup truck pulls in behind my car.

Relief floods through me, followed immediately by a different kind of tension as Carson steps out of the driver's side, his tall frame silhouetted against his headlights.

"Car trouble?" he calls, walking toward me with that easy, loose-limbed stride of his.

"Just a flat," I reply, trying to sound casual, like I'm not secretly pleased to see him. "Nothing I can't handle."

He reaches me, looking down at the tire and the wrench in my hand with barely concealed amusement. "Clearly."

"I was doing fine before you showed up," I lie, tossing my hair back from my face. "But feel free to help if you're so inclined."

"Wouldn't dream of interfering with your mechanical expertise," he says, but he's already taking the wrench from my hands, our fingers brushing, and I try to ignore the sparks that fly between us. "Just happened to be driving by."

"Just happened to be driving by this specific stretch of road at this specific time?" I arch an eyebrow. "What a coincidence."

He grins, that crooked half-smile that does something alarming to my insides. "Isn't it, though?"

The truth is, these coincidences have been happening with increasing frequency over the past few months, ever since the night at the Rusty Spur when Atlee first pointed out the way he looked at me. Since he was held hostage by Noah, he's been showing up more and more in places that I might be.

And each time, there's that same electricity between us, that same flirtation that never quite crosses the line into something more serious.

"So," he says, crouching down to position the jack under my car, muscles flexing beneath his worn T-shirt. "Where were you headed this fine evening?"

"Dinner at Jesse and Aubree's," I tell him, hugging my arms

around myself against the evening chill. "Wedding shower planning committee."

He glances up at me. "For Devlin and Atlee?"

"And both of them," I confirm. "They're doing a joint thing, since the weddings are only a month apart."

"Romantic," he comments, turning his attention back to the tire. "Two brothers marrying two best friends."

"Three months ago, I'd have called it crazy," I admit. "Now it seems like the most natural thing in the world."

He makes a noise in the back of his throat that might be affirmation, or not. Carson works in silence for a moment, the only sounds the chirping of crickets and the metallic clinking of the lug nuts as he removes them one by one.

"You ever think about it?" he asks suddenly.

"Think about what?"

"Marriage. Family. The whole white picket fence deal."

The question catches me off guard. "Sometimes," I answer cautiously. "When I'm not drowning in briefs and depositions."

He nods, as if I've confirmed something for him. "You'd make a good mom."

"You don't know that," I say, unsure why his words make my heart race. "You barely know me."

He looks up at me again, his expression serious now. "I know more than you think, Lennon."

There's something in his tone, something that makes me wonder what exactly he means. But before I can ask, he's back to focusing on the tire, the spare now in position as he tightens the lug nuts with practiced efficiency.

"Almost done," he says, standing and dusting off his hands on his jeans. "You'll be on your way to that dinner in no—"

The crack of a gunshot cuts through the evening stillness, followed immediately by the ping of a bullet hitting metal somewhere near us. Carson reacts before I can even process what's happening, tackling me to the ground behind my car.

"What the—" I start, but he covers my mouth with his hand, his body shielding mine as another shot rings out, then another.

"When I say go, we run for my truck," he whispers, his breath warm against my ear. "Stay low, zigzag if you can. Ready?"

I nod, too stunned to argue. His hand moves from my mouth to grasp mine.

"Go!"

We sprint toward his truck, bullets kicking up dirt at our feet. Carson practically throws me into the passenger seat before diving across the hood and into the driver's side. The engine roars to life, and we're peeling away in a spray of gravel, tires screeching as he executes a hairpin turn back toward the main road.

"What the hell was that?" I gasp when I finally find my voice. "Who's shooting at us?"

Carson's knuckles are white on the steering wheel, his jaw clenched tight. "I was hoping you could tell me. Anyone with a reason to want you dead, Lennon?"

The question is so absurd I almost laugh, except for the deadly seriousness in his expression. "I'm a paralegal, not a mob boss," I say. "Why would anyone want to shoot me?"

"You tell me," he says, eyes constantly checking the rearview mirror. "Any cases you're working on that might have pissed someone off?"

I start to shake my head, then pause. "There's this thing Shawn and I have been investigating."

Carson's head snaps toward me. "What kind of thing?"

"I can't exactly tell you, just something that we've been building quietly."

"How quietly?"

"Just Shawn and me," I say. "And whoever just tried to kill us, apparently."

Carson mutters something under his breath that sounds like a curse. "We need to get you somewhere safe. Somewhere they won't look."

I notice we're not heading toward Grizzly River Ranch anymore, but in the opposite direction. "Where are we going?"

"Dark Skies Ranch," he answers grimly. "My place. It's secure, remote, and no one would think to look for you there."

"I need to call Atlee," I say, reaching for my phone. "She'll be worried sick."

"Use my phone," Carson says, handing me his. "Better reception. But don't tell her where you are. Not yet. Not until we know what we're dealing with."

As I dial my sister's number, I realize we've crossed some invisible line. Whatever careful dance Carson and I have been doing these past months, whatever walls I've built to keep him at a safe distance, they're gone now, shattered by gunfire and the knowledge that someone wants me dead.

"You're staying at Dark Skies until we figure out what the hell is going on," Carson says, his tone leaving no room for argument. "I'm not letting anything happen to you, Lennon. Not on my watch."

The fierce protectiveness in his voice should irritate me. I've spent my whole life taking care of myself, taking care of Atlee, needing no one. Instead, I find myself oddly comforted by it, by the certainty in his words.

"Fine," I agree, watching the dark landscape rush past outside the window. "But this is temporary."

He glances over at me, that half-smile making another appearance despite the gravity of our situation. "We'll see about that."

As Dark Skies Ranch appears in the distance, a sprawling structure silhouetted against the night sky, I can't shake the feeling that nothing about this, about us, is going to be temporary.

And for once in my life, that thought doesn't terrify me nearly as much as it should.

A LOOK AT BOOK THREE
SPURRED

Some secrets are worth dying for... but this cowboy won't let that happen.

When Lennon Walsh is nearly gunned down on the side of the highway, the last man she expects to come to her rescue is Carson Nelson—the youngest of the notorious Nelson brothers, and the cocky cowboy who once stood her up and walked away.

Carson pulls her into his truck and takes her to Dark Skies Ranch, promising to keep her safe. Lennon knows she shouldn't rely on anyone. She survived neglectful parents, raised her sister, and built a career as a paralegal by standing on her own. Trust has never been her strong suit.

But being under Carson's protection changes things. The way he watches her. The heat he doesn't try to hide. And the fragile control behind his charm, shaped by his own demons. When she pushes him away, he pushes right back.

With someone hunting her and secrets tied to her job closing in, Lennon is forced to decide what's more dangerous—staying guarded, or falling for a younger man who refuses to let her fight alone.

AVAILABLE MAY 2026

Laramie Briscoe is the *USA Today* and *Wall Street Journal* bestselling author of over thirty books, with sales of over half a million copies.

Since self-publishing her first book in May of 2013, Laramie has appeared on the Top 100 Bestselling E-books Lists on Amazon Kindle, Apple Books, Barnes & Noble, and Kobo. Her books have been known to make readers laugh and cry. They are guaranteed to be emotional, steamy reads.

When she's not writing alpha males who seriously love their women, she loves spending time with friends, reading, and marathoning shows on Netflix. Married to her high school sweetheart, Laramie lives in Bowling Green, Kentucky, with her husband (the Travel Coordinator) and an adorable dog named Gus.

www.laramiebriscoe.net

www.ingramcontent.com/pod-product-compliance
Lightning Source LLC
LaVergne TN
LVHW041250110826
845146LV00005BA/1333